WHAT
KATY DID

— Susan M. Coolidge —

WHAT
KATY DID

Published in this edition 1997 by Peter Haddock Ltd,
Pinfold Lane, Bridlington, East Yorkshire YO16 5BT
Reprinted 1999

© 1997 This arrangement, text and illustrations,
Children's Leisure Products Limited, David Dale House,
New Lanark, Scotland

© Original text John Kennett

Illustrated by Mike Taylor (Simon Girling Associates)

ISBN 0 7105 0939 1

Printed and bound in India

Contents

To the Reader

I am sure you will have seen a film, or watched a programme on TV, that has been made from some famous book. If you enjoyed the film or programme, you may have decided to read the book.

Then what happens? You get the book and, it's more than likely, you get a shock as well! You turn ten or twenty pages, and nothing seems to *happen*. Where are all the lively people and exciting incidents? When, you say, will the author get down to telling the story? In the end you will probably throw the book aside and give it up. Now, why is that?

Well, perhaps the author was writing for adults and not for children. Perhaps the book was written a long time ago, when people had more time for reading and liked nothing better than a book that would keep them entertained for weeks.

We think differently today. That's why I've taken some of these wonderful books, and retold them for you. If you enjoy them in this shorter form, then I hope that when you are older you will go back to the original books, and enjoy all the more the wonderful stories they have to tell.

About the Author

Susan Coolidge was a popular writer of many kinds of books and poems, but she is best remembered and loved for her children's stories.

Her real name was Sarah Chauncey Woolsey, and she was a niece of Theodore Dwight Woolsey, who was President of Yale University from 1846 till 1871. She was born in 1845 at Cleveland, Ohio, in the United States of America, and died at Newport, Rhode Island, in 1905.

Chapter One
The Carr Family

Katy's name was Katy Carr. She lived in the town of Burnet, which is a small place in America. The house she lived in stood on the edge of the town. It was a large, square, white house, with green blinds, and a porch in front with roses growing over it. On one side of the house was an orchard; on the other side were wood-piles and barns, and an ice-house for keeping ice frozen during the summer.

There were six of the Carr children—four girls and two boys. Katy, the oldest, was just twelve; little Phil, the youngest, was four; and the rest fitted in between.

Their father was a doctor, and they hadn't any mother. She had died when Phil was a baby, four years before. Only Katy could remember anything about her at all.

In place of a mother, there was Aunt Izzie, the doctor's sister, who had come to take care of them all after mother went away on that long journey. She was a small, thin woman, sharp-faced and rather fussy about everything, and not very good at understanding children or the things they like to do.

The doctor wasn't like that. He wanted the children to be bold and hardy, and liked to see them climbing and playing rough games, in spite of the bumps and torn clothes which came from it.

Now, I want to show you the little Carrs and I don't think I could pick a better time than one Saturday morning when five out of the six were perched on top of the ice-house, like chickens on a coop.

Clover, next in age to Katy, sat in the middle. She was a sweet dumpling of a girl with thick pig-tails of light brown hair and short-sighted blue eyes which seemed to hold tears just ready to fall from under the blue. Little Phil sat next to Clover, and she held him tight with her arms. Then came Elsie, a thin child of eight, with eyes that were as bright and quick as a bird's.

Dorry and Joanna sat on the two ends of the roof's ridge-pole. Dorry was six years old; a pale, pudgy boy with rather a solemn face and smears of jam on the sleeve of his jacket. Joanna, whom the children called "Johnnie", was a square, splendid child, a year younger than Dorry; she had big eyes and a wide rosy mouth which always looked ready to laugh. These two were great friends, though Dorry seemed like a girl who had got into boy's clothes by mistake, and Johnnie like a boy who, in a fit of fun, had borrowed his sister's frock.

Now, as they all sat there chattering, the window above opened, a glad shriek was heard, and Katy's head popped out. In her hand she held a bundle of stockings, which she waved in the air.

"I've finished the darning," she cried. "Aunt Izzie says

we may go now. Are you tired out waiting? I couldn't help it, the holes were *so* big, and took so long. Hurry up, Clover, and get the things! Cecy and I will be down in a minute."

The children jumped up gladly, and slid down the roof. Clover fetched a couple of baskets from the wood-shed. Elsie ran for her kitten. Dorry and Johnnie armed themselves with two big sticks. Just as they were ready, the side-door banged, and Katy and Cecy Hall came into the yard.

I must tell you about Cecy. She lived in the house next door. Between the houses there was only a green hedge, with no gate, so that Cecy spent two thirds of her time at Dr Carr's, and was just like one of the family. She was a neat, pink-and-white girl, with light shiny hair which always kept smooth, and slim hands which never looked dirty.

How different from poor Katy!

Katy's hair was always untidy; her dresses were always catching on nails and "tearing themselves"; and, in spite of her age and size, she was always in and out of mischief. She was also the *longest* girl that was ever seen. What she did to make herself grow so, nobody could tell; but there she was, already up above father's ear, and half a head taller than poor Aunt Izzie.

Katy's days flew like the wind. When she wasn't studying lessons, or sewing and darning with Aunt Izzie— which she hated very much— there were so many de-

lightful schemes rioting in her brains that all she wished for was ten pairs of hands to carry them out. Her active mind was always getting her into scrapes. She was fond of building castles in the air and of dreaming of the time when something she had done would make her famous, so that everybody would hear of her and want to know her. She'd not made up her mind what this wonderful thing was to be, but she was always planning how, by and by, she would be beautiful and beloved and as full of grace as an angel.

A great deal would have to happen to Katy before that time came, she imagined. Her eyes, which were black, would have to turn blue; her nose would have to lengthen and straighten, and her mouth—which was much too large at the moment—would have to be made over into a sort of rosy button. Meantime, she forgot about her face as much as she could and got on with all the exciting things there were to do.

And now that you've met Katy and the others, let's follow them and see what they were up to on this fine Saturday morning....

Chapter Two
The Camp

The place to which the children were going was a sort of marshy thicket at the bottom of a field near the house. In winter the place was all damp and boggy, so that nobody went there excepting cows, who don't mind getting their feet wet; but in summer the water dried away so that it was all fresh and green, and full of wild roses and birds' nests. Narrow, winding paths ran here and there, made by the cattle as they wandered to and fro. This place the children called their camp, and to them it seemed as wild and endless and as full of adventure as any forest of fairyland.

They had to get to it through a wooden fence. Katy and Cecy climbed this with a hop, skip, and a jump, while the smaller ones scrambled underneath. Once past the fence they all began to run till they reached the edge of the wood.

They halted.

"Which path shall we go in by?" asked Clover.

"The Path of Peace," said Katy, and led the way into the thicket.

The Path of Peace got its name because of its dark-ness and coolness. High bushes almost met over it, and

trees kept it shady even in the middle of the day. A sort
of wild flower grew there, which the children called
Pollypods because they didn't know the real name. They
stayed a long while picking bunches of these flowers; so
that before they had gone through Toadstool Avenue,
Rabbit Hollow, and the rest, the sun was just over their
heads and it was noon.

"I'm getting hungry," said Dorry.

Dorry never liked to be kept waiting for his meals, but
there was something that had to be done before he could
eat.

"You'll have to wait until the camp is ready," cried the
little girls, and all of them set to work to build their
camp.

It did not take long, for it was made of boughs hung
over skipping-ropes which were tied to the stems of trees.

When it was done they all cuddled in underneath. It
was a very small camp—just big enough to hold them
and the baskets, and the kitten. I don't think there would
have been room for anybody else, not even another kitten.

Katy sat in the middle and untied the lid of the largest
basket. She lifted it, while all the rest peeped eagerly to
see what was inside.

First came a great many ginger cakes. These were carefully laid on the grass to keep till wanted. Buttered bis-
cuits came next—three apiece, with slices of cold lamb
laid in between; then a dozen hard-boiled eggs, and

last of all a layer of thick bread-and-butter sandwiched with corned beef.

How good everything tasted in that camp, with the fresh wind rustling the poplar leaves, sunshine and wood-smells about them, and the birds singing over-head! It was great fun. Each mouthful was a pleasure; and when the last crumb had gone, Katy opened the second basket, and there, delightful surprise! were seven little pies—fruit pies, baked in saucers—each with a brown top and crisp edge, which tasted like toffee and lemon-peel and all sorts of good things mixed up together.

Everybody shouted at the sight, and Johnnie and Dorry kicked their heels on the ground in the wildest of joy. Seven pairs of hands were held out towards the basket, seven sets of teeth were at once set to work.

Within two or three minutes every scrap of the pies had gone, and the whole party were happily and con-tentedly sticky.

"What shall we do now?" asked Clover.

"I don't know," replied Katy, dreamily.

She had left her seat and was half-lying on the low, crooked bough of a tree which hung almost over the children's heads.

"Let's play we're grown up," said Cecy, "and tell what we mean to do."

"All right," said Clover, "you begin. What do you mean to do?"

"I'm going to have lots of beautiful silk dresses," said

Cecy, "and I shall look good, and be very good, too. All the young men will want me to go and ride with them, but I shan't notice them at all because I shall always be teaching in Sunday-school, and visiting the poor. And one day, when I'm bending over a poor old woman and feeding her with currant jelly, a poet will come along and see me, and he'll go home and write a poem about me," finished Cecy triumphantly.

"Pooh!" said Clover. "I don't think there's much fun in that. *I'm* going to be a beautiful lady—the most beautiful lady in the world! And I'm going to live in a yellow castle, with a sun-house on the roof. My children will have a play-house up there. I shall wear gold or silver dresses every day, and diamond rings, and have white satin aprons to tie on when I'm dusting or doing anything dirty. In the middle of my back-yard there'll be a pond full of Eau de Cologne, and whenever I want any I shall just go out and dip a bottle in!"

"I'll have just the same," cried Elsie, who thought all this sounded very grand, "only my pond will be the biggest. I shall be a great deal beautifuller, too," she added.

"You can't," said Katy from overhead. "Clover is going to be the most beautiful lady in the world."

"But I'll be *more* beautiful than the most beautiful," cried Elsie.

"You can't!" shrieked the rest, and they all roared with laughter.

"What'll you be, Johnnie?" asked Clover.

"I don't know," said Johnnie simply. "I 'spect I'll just be me—only bigger!"

Dorry had more to say than that.

"I'm going to eat turkey every day," he said, "and batter-puddings with brown shiny tops. I shall be so big then that nobody will tell me three helpings are enough for a little boy."

"Oh, Dorry, you pig!" cried Katy, while the rest screamed with laughter.

"It's your turn, Katy," said Cecy. "What are you going to be when you're grown up?"

Katy frowned.

"I'm not sure," she replied. "I'll be beautiful, of course, and good if I can—only not so good as you, Cecy, because *I* think it would be fun to go and ride with the young gentlemen *sometimes*. And I'd like to have a large house with a splendiferous garden, and then you could all come and live with me, and Dorry could have turkey five times a day if he liked. And we'd have a machine to darn the stockings, and another machine to tidy the toy cupboards, and we'd never sew or knit, or do anything we didn't want to. That's what I'd like to *be*. Now I'll tell you what I mean to *do*."

"Isn't it the same thing?" asked Cecy.

"Oh, no!" replied Katy, "it's quite different. I mean to *do* something grand. I don't know what yet, but when I'm grown up I shall find out. Perhaps it'll be rowing

out in boats and saving people's lives, like that girl in
the book. Or perhaps I shall go and nurse in the hospi-
tal, like Florence Nightingale. Or if I don't do that, I'll
paint pictures, or sing, or scalp—sculp—what is it? You
know—make figures in marble. Anyhow, it shall be *something*. And when Aunt Izzie sees it, and reads about me
in the newspapers, she'll say, 'That dear child! I always
knew she'd turn out to be a credit to the family!' People
very often say, afterwards, that they 'always knew'," finished Katy, wisely.

"Oh, Katy, how wonderful!" sighed Clover, who believed in Katy as she did in the Bible.

"The newspapers wouldn't be silly enough to print
anything about *you*, Katy Carr," put in Elsie.

"Yes, they will!" cried Clover, and gave Elsie a push.

By and by John and Dorry trotted away on mysterious errands of their own.

"Wasn't Dorry funny about his turkey?" remarked
Cecy; and they all laughed again.

"If you promise not to tell," said Katy, "I'll let you see
his diary. He kept it once for almost two weeks, and
then gave it up. I found it this morning in the nursery
cupboard."

All of them promised, and Katy took the diary from
her pocket. It began thus:

"*March 12*—Have desidid to keep a dairy.

"*March 13*—Had roste befe for diner, and cabage, and
potato and appel sawse, and rice puding. I do not like

rice puding when it is like ours. Charley Slack's kind is
rele good. Jam and sirup for tea.

"*March 19*—Forgit what did. Johnnie and me saved
our pie to take to schule.

"*March 21*—Forgit what did. Appel crumberley for
diner. Did not get enuff.

"*March 24*—This is Sunday. Corn befe for diner. Stud-
ied my Bibel lesson. Aunt Issy said I was gredy. Have
desided not to think so much about things to ete. Wish
I was a beter boy Nothing pertikler for tea.

"*March 25*—Forgit what did.

"*March 27*—Forgit what did.

"*March 29*—Played.

"*March 31*—Forgit what did.

"*April 1*—Have dissided not to kepe a dairy enny
more."

Here ended the extracts; and it seemed as if only a
minute had passed since they stopped laughing over
them, when the long shadows began to fall and it was
time to go home and get ready for tea.

It was dreadful to have to pick up the empty baskets
and wander back, feeling that the long, delightful Saturday was nearly over, and that there wouldn't be another for a week—and a week of schooldays, at that....

Chapter Three

The Day of Scrapes

Katy and Clover and Cecy all went to Mrs Knight's school, which stood right at the other end of the town. It was a low, one-storey building, with a playground behind it. Next door, as luck would have it, was Miss Miller's school, with a yard behind it also. Only a high board fence separated the two playgrounds.

Mrs Knight was a stout, slow-moving woman. She had a face which made you think of a friendly and kind-hearted cow. Miss Miller, on the other hand, was tall and thin, had black eyes and corkscrew curls, and was always brisk and snappy.

A fierce and deadly rivalry raged between the two schools. The Knight girls, for some unknown reason, thought of themselves as young ladies who were a cut above the "Millerites", and took no pains to hide their opinion. The Millerites, for their part, returned like for like and were as aggravating as they knew how.

They spent their playtimes in making faces through the knot-holes in the fence, and over the top of it when they could get there, which wasn't an easy thing to do, as the fence was pretty high.

The Knight girls, also, were very good at making faces.

In their yard was a wooden shed, with a climbable roof, which overlooked the rival playground, and upon this the girls used to sit in rows, turning up their noses at the enemy, and irritating them by jeering remarks.

One morning Katy was late for school. She could not find any of her things at home. Her algebra book, as she kept saying crossly, had "gone and lost itself", her slate was missing, and the string was off her sun-bonnet. She ran about, banging doors and searching for these things, till Aunt Izzie was quite out of patience.

"As for your algebra book," she said, "if it's that very dirty book with only one cover, and scribbled all over the leaves, you'll find it under the kitchen table. Phil was playing that it was a pig just now—and no wonder, I'm sure, for it looks good for nothing else. I can't think how you manage to get your school-books into such a mess. It's less than a month since your father got you a new algebra book, and look at it now—not fit to be carried about. I do wish you'd realize what books cost!"

Katy, meanwhile, had dropped to hands and knees and pulled her algebra book out from under the kitchen table. She straightened up, all red-faced and breathless.

"I don't know what's happened to your slate," Aunt Izzie went on, "but here's the bonnet-string."

She took it from her pocket.

"Oh, thank you!" cried Katy, hastily sticking it on with a pin.

"Katy Carr," almost screamed Aunt Izzie, "*what are you doing*? You're not leaving this house till I've sewn that string on properly."

It wasn't easy to "stand still and not fidget", with Aunt Izzie fussing away, and now and then, in a moment of forgetfulness, sticking her needle into one's chin. Katy bore it as well as she could, shifting all the time from one foot to another, and now and then uttering a little snort, like an impatient horse. The minute she was released, she rushed like a whirlwind to the gate, where Clover stood waiting.

"We'll have to run," gasped Katy, quite out of breath. "Aunt Izzie kept me. She's been so horrid!"

They did run as fast as they could, but time ran faster, and before they were half-way to school the town clock struck nine, and all hope was over. This vexed Katy very much, for, though often late, she was always eager to be early.

"There," she said, stopping short, "I shall just tell Aunt Izzie that it was her fault. It's too bad!"

From that moment, everything seemed to go wrong. Katy was in trouble all morning through. But the worst was yet to come....

As soon as the bell rang, Katy made a bolt for the yard, and was first up to the wood-house roof. Miss Miller's clock was about four minutes slower than Mrs Knight's, so the next playground was empty. It was a warm, breezy day, and as Katy sat there suddenly a

gust of wind came, seized her sun-bonnet, which was only half tied on, and whirled it across the roof. She made a grab for it, but was too late. It dropped over the edge of the roof, and Katy, clutching after it, saw it lying in a crumpled lilac heap in the very middle of the enemy's yard.

This, of course, was horrible!

Katy didn't really mind losing the bonnet, for she never bothered or cared what became of her clothes—but she didn't want to lose her bonnet to *the enemy,* for that was quite a different matter.

In another minute the Miller girls would be out. Katy knew what would happen then. She could see the hated foe dancing war-dances round the bonnet, pinning it on a pole, using it as a football, waving it over the fence, and otherwise treating it as Indians treat a captive taken in war.

Was Katy to stand for that?

Never! Better die first!

Without another thought, Katy set her teeth, slid down the roof, seized the fence, and with one bold leap vaulted into Miss Miller's yard.

Then two things happened almost at once. The bell rang for playtime in Miss Miller's school; and a little Millerite who sat by the window gave an excited squeal:

"There's Katy Carr in our playground!"

Out poured the Millerites, big and little. Their wrath at this daring invasion cannot be described. The *cheek*

of it! Howling with fury, they flocked through the door
and threw themselves upon Katy. She, however, was as
quick as they. She snatched up her bonnet, turned, hared
towards the fence, and was half-way up when the
Millerites surged upon her.

There are times when it is a fine thing to be tall. This
was one of them, for Katy's long legs and arms did her
a good turn. Nothing but a daddy-long-legs ever
climbed so fast or so wildly as she did now. In one second she had gained the top of the fence. Just as she
went over a Millerite seized her by the foot, and almost
dragged her shoe off.

Almost—but not quite. Katy gave a frantic kick and
had the pleasure of seeing her assailant go head over
heels backward, while, with a shriek of triumph, she
herself plunged headlong into a group of Knights.

They were standing open-mouthed, listening to the
uproar on the other side of the fence, and now stood
rooted to the spot at the sight of Katy returning alive
from the enemy camp.

You may imagine the fuss that followed!

The Knights were filled with pride and triumph. Katy
was the heroine of the school. She was made to tell her
story over and over again, while rows of jeering girls sat
on the wood-house roof to crow over the unhappy
Millerites.

All this was more than they could stand, and several
of them began clambering up the fence, to hang over

and scream insults at the Knights. But not for long, because Clover, armed with a tack-hammer, was lifted up in the arms of one of the tall girls to rap the knuckles of the Millerites as they came over the top. This she did with such goodwill that the Millerites were glad to drop down again, and mutter vengeance at a safe distance.

Altogether it was a great day for the school—a day to be remembered. As time went on, Katy, what with the excitement of her adventure, and of being praised and petted by the big girls, grew perfectly reckless, and hardly knew what she said or did.

It was this that brought about her downfall....

Chapter Four
The Game of Rivers

A good many of the girls lived too far from school to go home at noon, and so they brought their lunches in baskets and stayed all day. Katy and Clover did this.

After the dinners were eaten, a whole group of girls went to play something in the schoolroom, and Katy's unlucky star put it into her head to invent a new game.

It was called the Game of Rivers. This is how it was played. Each girl took the name of a river and laid out for herself a path through the room, winding among the desks and benches and making a low, roaring sound like the noise of tumbling water. Cecy was the Platte; Marianne Brookes, a tall girl, the Mississippi; Alice Blair, the Ohio; and so on. They had to run into each other once in a while, because, as Katy said, "rivers do".

Katy herself was "Father Ocean". Growling horribly, she raged up and down the platform where Mrs Knight usually sat. Every now and then, when the others were at the far end of the room, she would suddenly cry out, "Now for a meeting of the waters!" whereupon all the rivers, bouncing, pounding, scrambling, screaming, would turn and run towards Father Ocean, while he roared louder than all of them put together, and made

short rushes up and down to show how his waves were crashing on a beach.

It was a fine game, a beautiful game—but it made such a noise as was never heard in the town of Burnet before or since! It was all screams and howls, and banging of furniture, and scraping of feet on an uncarpeted floor.

People going by stopped and stared, children cried, and an old lady asked why someone didn't run for a policeman.

Mrs Knight, coming back from dinner, was startled to see a crowd of people in front of her school. As she drew near, the sounds reached her, and then she became really frightened, for she thought somebody was being murdered inside.

She hurried in and threw open the door. Her eyes almost bolted from her head. The whole room was in an uproar: chairs were flung down, desks upset, and ink was streaming on the floor. In the midst of the ruin the frantic rivers were racing and screaming, and Father Ocean, with a face as red as fire, danced like a mad thing on the platform. . . .

Mrs Knight opened her mouth. She was, for a moment, almost unable to speak for horror— but she managed it.

"What does this mean?" she gasped.

Her voice was lost in the din, but one or two of the girls had already seen her at the door. One by one the

Rivers stood still, while Father Ocean brought his prancing to an end and slunk down from the platform.

The noise died away.

Then, in a flash, each girl saw what a sorry state the room was in; each realized what an awful thing she had done. The timid ones cowered behind their desks, the bold ones tried to look as if they had played no part in it; and to make matters worse, the girls who had gone home to dinner began to return, staring at the scene of the disaster and asking in whispers what had been going on.

Mrs Knight rang the bell. When the school had come to order, she had the desks and chairs picked up, while she herself brought cloths to sop the ink from the floor.

All this was done in dreadful silence.

When all was in order again, and the girls had taken their seats, Mrs Knight made a short speech .

"Never in all my life," she said, "have I been so shocked. I would never have believed that you could act in such a disgraceful manner, even to the extent of alarming people who were going by. I am deeply shocked. Your behaviour was a dreadful example to set, and I hope that you are sorry. I think you must be— sorry and ashamed. I shall, of course, have to punish you for what you have done, but I wish to think before I decide what form that punishment shall take. Meantime, I should like all of you to think it over seriously; and if anyone feels that she is more to blame than the

others, now is the moment to stand up and tell me so."

There was a little silence. Katy's heart gave a great thump. Then she rose bravely.

"I made up the game, Mrs Knight," she said, "and I was Father Ocean."

Mrs Knight looked astonished, glared at her for a minute, and then said: "Very well, Katy, sit down."

Katy sat, feeling more ashamed than ever, but glad that she had told the truth.

The afternoon was long and hard. Mrs Knight did not smile once; the lessons dragged; and Katy felt terribly miserable.

When school was over, Mrs Knight rose and said:

"The girls who took part in the game this afternoon are to stay behind."

All the others went away and shut the door behind them. It was a horrible moment.

Mrs Knight talked to them for a long time. She made it very clear just how wrongly they had behaved. Their punishment, she said, would be the loss of their play-time for three weeks to come. Then all the girls except Katy were sent on their way. Mrs Knight called Katy up to her desk and said a few words to her specially. She was not too hard, but Katy was so overcome by this time that before long she was weeping like a waterspout.

She sobbed, in fact, nearly all the way home. Luckily, Aunt Izzie was out, and Katy had bathed her face by

the time she got back, so that she looked herself again.

For a wonder, Dr Carr was at home that evening. After the little ones had gone to bed, Katy sat on his knee and told him the whole story.

"Why is it that some days seem so unlucky?" she asked him. "Today began all wrong, and everything that happened in it was wrong. If Aunt Izzie hadn't kept me in the morning, I shouldn't have been late, and then I shouldn't have been cross, and then *perhaps* I shouldn't have got in my other scrapes."

"What made Aunt Izzie keep you?"

"To sew on the string of my bonnet."

"But how did it happen that the string was off?"

"Well," said Katy slowly, "I suppose that was *my* fault. It came off last Tuesday, and I hadn't fastened it on."

"So you see we must go back before Aunt Izzie for the beginning of this unlucky day of yours. Did you ever hear the old saying about 'For the want of a nail the shoe was lost'?"

"No—tell it to me!" cried Katy.

So Dr Carr repeated:

"For the want of a nail the shoe was lost,
For the want of a shoe the horse was lost,
For the want of a horse the rider was lost,
For the want of the rider the battle was lost,
For the want of the battle the kingdom was lost,
And all for want of a horse-shoe nail."

"Oh, Father," exclaimed Katy, giving him a great hug

as she got off his knee, "I see what you mean! Who would have thought such a little speck of a thing as not sewing on my string could have made such a difference? But I'll remember what you've said, and I shan't get into any more scrapes. You'll see—I shan't forget!"

At that moment she meant what she said—but she *did* forget, and did get into another scrape, and that not later than the very next Monday.

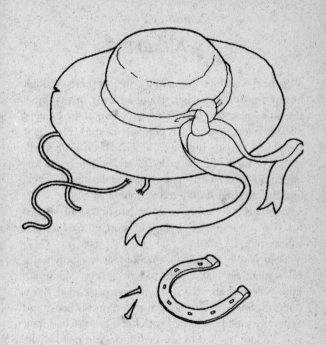

Chapter Five
Kikeri

This next Monday was a rainy one, so there couldn't be any outdoor play when school was over. By that time, the little ones, who had been cooped up in the nursery all afternoon, had grown perfectly riotous. Phil, as it happened, was not quite well, and had been given medicine. The medicine was called *Elixir Pro*. The bottle was large and black, with a paper label tied round its neck, and the children shuddered at sight of it.

Phil made a great fuss when he had to take his spoonful. It was a long time before he stopped roaring and spluttering.

When play began again, the dolls, as was only natural, were taken ill also—and so was "Pikery", Johnnie's little yellow chair, which she always pretended was a doll too. She kept an old apron tied on his back, and generally took him to bed with her—not *into* bed, that is, but close by, tied to the bed-post. And now, as she told the others, Pikery was very sick indeed. He must have some medicine.

"It must be black and out of a bottle," she said, "or it won't do any good at all."

After thinking a moment, she trotted quietly across

the passage into Aunt Izzie's room. The others were
delighted, when she marched back with the bottle of
Elixir Pro in one hand and the cork in the other. They
watched her pour a large dose on to Pikery's wooden
seat.

"There, there! My poor boy," she said, patting his
shoulder—I mean his arm. "Swallow it down. It'll do
you good."

Just then Aunt Izzie came in and saw, to her dismay, a
long trickle of something dark and sticky running down
on to the carpet. It was Pikery's medicine, which he
had refused to swallow.

"What's that?" she asked sharply.

"My baby's sick," faltered Johnnie, showing the bottle
in her hand.

Aunt Izzie rapped her over the knuckles, and told her
that she was a very naughty child, whereupon Johnnie
pouted and cried a little. Aunt Izzie wiped up the mess
and took away the elixir, saying that she "never knew
anything like it—things always went wrong on Mon-
days . . . ."

A little after that, a dreadful screaming was heard.
People came rushing from all parts of the house to see
what was wrong, and found that the nursery door was
locked on the inside. Nobody could get in.

Aunt Izzie called through the key-hole to have it
opened. Elsie, sobbing violently, explained that Dorry
had locked the door, and now the key wouldn't turn

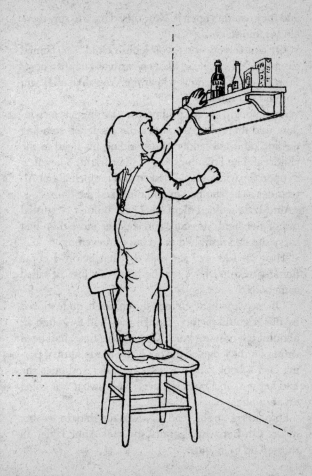

and they couldn't open it. Now they'd have to stay there always and starve!

"Of course you won't, you foolish child!" exclaimed Aunt Izzie. "Dear, dear, what on earth will happen next? Stop crying, Elsie, do you hear me? You shall all be got out in a few minutes."

Sure enough, the next thing was a rattling at the window, and there was Alexander, the gardener, standing outside on a tall ladder and nodding his head at the children. The little ones forgot their fright. They flew to open the window, and frisked and jumped about Alexander as he climbed in and unlocked the door.

Aunt Izzie scolded them all. They couldn't be trusted out of her sight, she said, and she was more than half sorry she had promised to go out that evening.

"How do I know," she ended, "that before I come home you won't have set the house on fire, or killed somebody?"

"Oh, no we won't!" chimed the children, quite moved by this frightful picture, though they had forgotten all about it ten minutes later. Katy, all this time, had been sitting on the ledge of the bookcase in the library, poring over a book. She was a great reader and once she had her nose in a book she never knew what was going on about her.

This afternoon she read till it was too dark to see any more. On her way upstairs she met Aunt Izzie, all dressed up to go out.

"Where *have* you been, Katy?" she said. "I've been calling you for the last half-hour."

"Oh! Sorry! I didn't hear you."

Her aunt gave a sniff.

"I'm going out with Mrs Hall," she said. "There's a meeting we have to attend. Now, if Cecy comes over as usual, you must send her home early. All of you must be in bed by nine at the latest."

"Yes, Auntie," said Katy, thinking how jolly it was to have Aunt Izzie go out for once.

Once their aunt had gone off, all the children felt a sense of novelty and freedom, which was dangerous as well as pleasant. Not that Katy meant any mischief. Like all excitable people, she never did *mean* to go wrong. All might have gone well that evening, had it not been that after Cecy had arrived they fell to talking about "Kikeri".

This was a game they had played a lot a year before. They'd invented it themselves, and chosen for it this queer name out of an old fairy story. It was a sort of mixture of Blind-man's-buff and Tag—only instead of anyone's eyes being bandaged, they all played in the dark. One of the children would stay out in the hall, which was dimly lighted from the stairs, while the others hid themselves in the nursery. When all were hidden, they would call out "Kikeri" as a signal for the one in the hall to come in and find them. Of course, coming from the light he could see nothing, while the others could see only dimly. It was very exciting to crouch in a cor-

ner and watch the dark figure stumbling about and feeling to right and left, while every now and then somebody, just escaping his clutches, would slip past and gain the hall, which was "Freedom Castle". Whoever was caught had to take the place of the catcher.

For a long time this game had been the delight of the Carr children; but so many bruises and scratches came of it, and so many of the nursery things were thrown down and broken, that at last Aunt Izzie had said that it should not be played any more.

This was almost a year since, but talking of it now put it into their heads to want to try it again.

"After all, we didn't promise," said Cecy.

"No, and it wasn't *Father* who said we mustn't play it!" added Katy.

Their minds were made up. They all went upstairs. Dorry and Johnnie, though half undressed, were allowed to join in the game. Philly was fast asleep in another room.

It was certainly splendid fun. Once, Clover climbed up on to the mantelpiece and sat there, and when Katy, who was finder, groped about a little more wildly than usual, she caught hold of Clover's foot and couldn't imagine where it came from. Dorry got a hard knock and cried; Katy's dress caught on a cupboard handle and was frightfully torn; but these were too much affairs of every day to interfere in the least with the pleasures of Kikeri. The fun and frolic seemed to grow greater

the longer they played. Time went on much faster than any of them dreamed.

And then, in the midst of the noise, there came a sound—the sharp slam of the carriage door at the side entrance. Aunt Izzie had come home!

Oh, the dismay and confusion of that moment!

Cecy slipped downstairs like an eel, and tore along the path which led to her home. Her mother, who had been out with Aunt Izzie, stood chatting for a moment, and might have been struck by the fact that a bang came from her own front door. She did not notice, however. When she went upstairs there were Cecy's clothes neatly folded on a chair, and Cecy herself in bed, fast asleep, only with a little more colour than usual in her cheeks.

In the meantime, Aunt Izzie was on *her* way upstairs—while panic reigned in the nursery. Katy fled to her own room and scrambled into bed as quickly as she could. The others found it much harder to get to bed. There were so many of them, all getting in each other's way, and they had no lamp to see by. Dorry and Johnnie popped under the clothes half dressed, Elsie hid, and Clover, too late for anything and hearing Aunt Izzie's step outside the door, fell on her knees, with her face buried in a chair, and began to say her prayers very hard indeed.

The door opened. Aunt Izzie stood there, a candle in her hand, quite astonished at the sight. She sat down, rather grimly, and waited for Clover to get through.

Clover, for her part, didn't dare to get through, but kept on repeating the same little prayers over and over again, in a sort of despair.

At last Aunt Izzie said very grimly: "All right, Clover. That will do. You can get up!"

Clover rose, hanging her head in shame. Aunt Izzie at once began to undress her, and while doing so asked so many questions that before long she had got at the truth of the whole matter. She gave Clover a sharp scolding, left her to wash her tearful face, and went to the bed where Johnnie and Dorry lay fast asleep, snoring as hard and loud as they knew how.

There was something odd about the look of the bed. Aunt Izzie peered more closely and lifted the clothes—and there the two lay, half-dressed and with their school boots on.

Aunt Izzie pounced. The two were shaken out of bed to be slapped and scolded, and made to wash and undress while Aunt Izzie stood over them like a dragon.

Katy did not even pretend to be asleep when Aunt Izzie came to her room. She knew that she had done wrong. She was lying in bed, very miserable at having drawn the others into a scrape as well as herself. She felt so unhappy, indeed, that when she cried herself to sleep it was more because of her own thoughts than because she had been scolded.

She cried even harder the next day, for Dr Carr talked to her more seriously than he had ever done before. He

reminded her of the time when her mother died, and of how she had said: "Katy must be a mother to the little ones when she grows up." And he asked her if she didn't think the time was coming for her to begin to take this place towards the children.

Poor Katy! She sobbed as if her heart would break at this, and though she made no promises, I think she was never quite so thoughtless again after that day.

Chapter Six
Katy's Friends

Katy came bursting into the house one afternoon.

"Aunt Izzie," she cried, "may I ask Imogen Clark to spend the day here on Saturday?"

"Who on earth is Imogen Clark?" demanded her aunt. "I never heard the name before."

"Oh, the *loveliest* girl! She's been going to Mrs Knight's school only a little while, but we're the greatest friends. You can't think how I love her!" said Katy fondly.

"No, I can't," Aunt Izzie replied tartly. "I never could see into these sudden friendships of yours, Katy, and I'd rather you wouldn't invite this Imogen, or whatever her name is, till I've had a chance to ask somebody about her."

Katy clasped her hands in despair.

"Oh, Aunt Izzie!" she cried. "Imogen knows that I came in to ask you, and she's standing at the gate this moment, waiting to hear what you say. Please let me, just this once! I shall be so dreadfully ashamed if you don't."

Aunt Izzie was moved by the wretchedness of Katy's face.

"Well," she said, "if you've asked her already, it's no

use my saying no, I suppose. But, remember that it's not to happen again. Your father is very particular about whom you make friends with. He has to be. Remember how Mrs Spenser turned out!"

Poor Katy! Ever since she began to walk and talk her "dear friends" had been one of the jokes of the family. Her father once started to keep a list of them, but the number grew so great that he gave it up in despair. First on the list was a small Irish child....

Her name was Marianne O'Riley. She lived in a street which Katy passed on her way to school. Marianne used always to be making sand-pies in front of her mother's house, and Katy, who was then about five years old, often stopped to help her. Katy grew so fond of her new friend that she made up her mind to adopt her as her own little girl, and bring her up in a safe and hidden corner.

She told Clover of this plan, but nobody else. The two children, full of their delightful secret, began to save pieces of bread and cake, and to collect fruit, which they hid away in the attic. They also made a bed in a big empty box, with cotton quilts and the dolls' pillows. When all was ready, Katy told Marianne of her plan, and easily persuaded her to run away to her new "home".

"We won't tell father and mother till she's quite grown up," Katy said to Clover, "then we'll bring her downstairs. Won't they be surprised!"

Marianne was easily smuggled into the house and up to the attic. For a whole day all went well. Marianne sat in her wooden box, ate all the apples and cakes that were given to her, and was happy enough. The two children took turns to steal away and play with the "baby", as they called Marianne, though she was a great deal bigger than Clover.

But when night came on, and Katy and Clover were put to bed, Marianne began to think that the attic was a dreadful place. She bore the silence and the dimness as long as she could, but when at last a rat began to scratch in the wall close beside her, she screamed at the top of her voice.

"What's that?" said the startled Dr Carr, who had just come in and was on his way upstairs.

"It sounds as if it came from the attic," said Mrs Carr, for this was before she died. "One of the children must have got out of bed and wandered upstairs in her sleep."

They both rushed to the nursery, where Katy and Clover lay fast asleep. The puzzled doctor took a candle and went as fast as he could to the attic, where the yells were growing terrific. When he reached the top of the stairs, the cries ceased. He looked about. Nothing was to be seen at first, then a little head appeared over the edge of a big wooden box, and a piteous voice sobbed out:

"Ah, Miss Katy, and indeed I can't be stayin' any longer. There's rats here."

"Who on earth are *you*?" asked the amazed doctor.

"Sure, I'm Miss Katy's baby. But I don't want to be a baby any longer. I want to go home and see my mother."

I don't think Dr Carr ever laughed so hard in his life as when he got to the bottom of the story and found that Katy and Clover had been "adopting" a child. But he was very kind to poor Marianne, and carried her downstairs to the nursery. There, in a bed close to the other children, she soon forgot her troubles and fell asleep.

The sisters were delighted when they woke up in the morning and found their baby asleep beside them. But their joy was speedily turned to tears. After breakfast, Dr Carr carried Marianne home to her mother, who was in a great fright over her disappearance, and explained that the attic plan must be given up.

After that, Katy had many more "friends". I can't begin to tell you how many, in fact. There was a dust-man and a steam-boat captain, and even a thief in the town jail, under whose window Katy used to stand, saying: "I'm so sorry for you, poor man!" and "Have you got any little girls like me?" in the most piteous way.

But of all Katy's strange friends, Mrs Spenser, of whom Aunt Izzie had spoken, was the strangest.

She was a mysterious lady whom nobody ever saw. Her husband was a handsome, rather bad-looking man, who had come from parts unknown, and rented a small house in Burnet. He didn't seem to work at anything

very much, and he was away from home a great deal. His wife was said to be an invalid, and people shook their heads and wondered how the poor woman got on all alone in the house, while her husband was away.

Katy, of course, was too young to understand these whispers, but she was very taken by the romance of the closed door and the lady whom nobody saw. She used to stop and stare at the windows, and wonder what was going on inside, till at last it seemed as if she *must* know.

One day she took some flowers and marched boldly into Mrs Spenser's yard.

She tapped at the front door. Nobody answered. She tried the door. It was locked, so she trudged round to the back of the house. As she passed the side door, she saw that it was open a little way. She knocked for the third time, and, as no one came, she went in, passed through a little hall, and began to tap at all the inside doors.

There seemed to be no one in the house. Katy peeped into the kitchen first. It was bare and untidy. All sorts of used dishes were standing about. Mr Spenser's boots lay in the middle of the floor. There were dirty glasses on the table. On the mantelpiece was a platter with meatbones on it. Dust lay thick over everything, and the whole house looked as if it hadn't been lived in for at least a year.

Katy tried several other doors, all of which were locked, and then she went upstairs. As she stood on the

top step, grasping her flowers, a feeble voice called from a bedroom:

"Who's there?"

It was Mrs Spenser. She was lying on her bed, which was very tossed and tumbled, as if it hadn't been made up that morning. The room was as untidy and dirty as the rest of the house, and Mrs Spenser's dressing gown and night-cap were by no means clean, though her face was sweet and she had beautiful curling hair which fell all over the pillow. She was ill, Katy could see, and the girl felt sorrier for her than she had ever done for anybody in her life.

"Who are you, child?" asked Mrs Spenser.

"I'm Dr Carr's little girl," answered Katy, going straight up to the bed. "I came to bring you some flowers."

She laid her bouquet on the dirty sheet.

Mrs Spenser seemed to like the flowers. She took them up and smelled them for a long time, without speaking.

"How did you get in?" she said at last.

"The door was open," answered Katy, "and they said you were ill, so I thought perhaps you would like me to come and see you."

"You're a kind little girl," said Mrs Spenser, and gave her a hug and a kiss.

After this Katy used to go every day. Sometimes Mrs Spenser would be up and moving feebly about; but more often she was in bed, and Katy could sit beside her.

The house never looked a bit better than it did that first day, but after a while Katy used to brush Mrs Spenser's hair and wash her face with the corner of a towel.

Mrs Spenser never spoke of her husband, and Katy never saw him except once, when she was so frightened that for several days she dared not go near the house. Then she heard that he had gone off again, and started going back once more.

Mrs Spenser cried when she saw her.

"I thought you weren't coming any more," she said.

Katy was touched and flattered at having been missed, and after that she never lost a day.

Aunt Izzie was very much worried by all this, but Dr Carr would not interfere. He said it was a case where grown people could do nothing, and if Katy was a comfort to the poor lady he was glad.

Then, one day, Katy stopped as usual on her way home from school. She tried the side door—and found it locked. The back door was locked also. All the blinds were shut tight. This was very puzzling.

As she stood in the yard a woman put her head out of a window of the next house.

"It's no use knocking," she said. "They've gone away."

"Gone away where?" asked Katy.

"Nobody knows," said the woman. "The gentleman came back in the middle of the night, and this morning, before light, he had a wagon at the door, and just put in the trunks and the sick lady, and drove off."

So Mrs Spenser went away, and Katy never saw her again.

In a few days it came out that Mr Spenser was a very bad man, and had been making false money—forging, as grown-ups called it. The police were searching for him to put him in jail, and that was the reason he had come back in such a hurry and carried off his poor wife.

Aunt Izzie, of course, was horrified when she heard this. She said it was a disgrace that Katy should have been visiting the wife of a criminal. Dr Carr only laughed. He told Aunt Izzie that he didn't think that kind of crime was catching, and, as for Mrs Spenser, she was much to be pitied.

Every now and then, when Aunt Izzie was really cross, she would drag up the affair of Mrs Spenser. Katy always felt badly when her aunt spoke unkindly of her poor sick friend. She had tears in her eyes now, as she walked to the gate, where Imogen Clark stood waiting.

Imogen was rather a pretty girl, with shiny brown hair, and a little round curl on each of her cheeks. These curls must have been fastened on with glue or tin tacks, one would think, for they never moved, however much she laughed or shook her head. She was quite a bright girl, but she had read so many stories that her brain was completely turned, and she lived in a world of her own making.

From this time on till the end of the week, the Carr

children talked of nothing but Imogen's visit and the
nice time they were all going to have.

On the Saturday, Imogen arrived about half-past ten.
She was all dressed up as if for a party, and wore coral
beads in her hair. The Carr children were quite daz-
zled by the appearance of their guest.

"Oh, Imogen," said simple Katy, "you look just like a
young lady in a story!"

Imogen tossed her head, and rustled her skirts about
more than ever. Somehow, with these fine clothes and
the fine manner she was putting on, she seemed a different person. She minced about and simpered and
lisped, and looked at herself in the glass, and was generally grown-up and airy. When Aunt Izzie spoke to
her, she fluttered and behaved so strangely that Clover
almost laughed outright; and even Katy was glad to
carry her away to play in the loft of the barn.

They all crossed the yard together. Imogen picked her
way daintily in her white satin slippers, but when she
saw that to get into the loft she would have to climb a
tall wooden post, with spikes driven into it about a foot
apart, she gave a shrill scream.

"Oh, not up there, darlings, not up *there*!" she cried.

"Oh, but do try!" begged Katy. "It's as easy as can be."

She went up and down half a dozen times to show
how easy it was, but Imogen wouldn't even try.

"Don't ask me," she said. "My nerves would never
stand it! Besides—my dress!"

"What made you wear it?" asked Philly, who was a plain-spoken child.

"I think she's a stupid girl," Johnnie whispered to Dorry. "Let's go off somewhere and play by ourselves."

So, one by one, the small fry crept away, leaving Katy and Clover to entertain the visitor by themselves. They tried dolls, but Imogen did not care for dolls. There seemed to be very little that Imogen *did* like. In the end, they went to the orchard, where their guest ate a great many plums and really seemed to enjoy herself at last. But when she could eat no more, a dreadful dullness fell over the party.

At last Imogen said:

"Don't you ever sit in the drawing-room?"

"The what?" asked Clover.

"The drawing-room," Imogen repeated.

"Oh, she means the parlour!" cried Katy. "No, we don't sit there except when Aunt Izzie has company for tea. It's all dark and poky, you know. It's much nicer to be out of doors."

"I'd like to go and sit there for a while," said Imogen. "My head aches dreadfully, being out here in this horrid sun."

Katy was at her wits' end to know what to do. They scarcely ever went into the parlour, and Aunt Izzie certainly would not want the children in there by themselves. On the other hand, it was dreadful to think that Imogen might go away and say: "Katy Carr isn't al-

lowed in the best room, even when she has company."

With a quaking heart, she led the way to the parlour.
She dared not open the blinds, so the room looked very
dark. She could just see Imogen's figure as she sat on
the sofa, and Clover twirling about uneasily on the pi-
ano-stool.

Imogen, who for the first time seemed comfortable,
now began to talk. Her talk was all about herself. Such
stories she told about the things which happened to her!
No one, it seemed, had ever had stranger adventures.
Gradually Katy and Clover got so interested that they
left their seats and crouched down close to the sofa,
listening open-mouthed to these stories. Katy forgot to
listen for Aunt Izzie. When the parlour door swung open,
she did not even notice it. Neither did she hear the front
door shut when her father came home for dinner.

Dr Carr, stopping in the hall to glance at his newspa-
per, heard the high-pitched voice running on in the
parlour. At first he hardly listened; then these words
caught his ear:

"Oh, girls, it was *lovely* ! I suppose *I did* look beautiful,
for I was all in white, with my hair let down and just
one rose, you know, here on the top. And he leaned
over me and said in a low, deep tone, 'Lady, I am a
brigand, but I feel the enchanting power of beauty. You
are free!'"

Dr Carr pushed the door open a little further. He heard
Katy's eager voice:

"Oh, *do* go on. What happened next?"

He left it there and went into the dining-room, where he found Aunt Izzie.

"Who on earth have the children got in the parlour?" he asked.

"The parlour!" cried Aunt Izzie wrathfully. "Why, what are they doing there?" Then going to the door, she called out: "Children, what are you doing in the parlour? Come out at once!"

"Imogen had a headache," faltered Katy, as the three girls came into the hall.

"I'm sorry to hear that," said Aunt Izzie grimly. "She's bilious, perhaps. Would you like some camphor or anything?"

"No, thank you," replied Imogen meekly enough, but afterwards she whispered to Katy:

"I don't think your aunt is very nice!"

Katy flushed.

"I don't think you're very polite to say so," she replied angrily.

"Oh, never mind, dear, don't take it to heart!" said Imogen sweetly. "We can't help having relations that are not nice, you know."

The visit was not turning out to be the success that Katy had expected. Father was very polite to Imogen at dinner, but he watched her closely, and Katy saw a comical twinkle in his eye, which she did not like.

"Aren't you glad she's gone?" whispered Clover, as they

stood at the gate together and watched Imogen walk down the street.

"Oh, Clover, how can you?" said Katy.

But she gave Clover a big hug, and I think in her heart she *was* glad.

"Katy," said Dr Carr next day, "you came into the room just now like your new friend Miss Clark."

Katy blushed.

"How? I don't know what you mean," she said feebly.

The doctor rose.

"Like this," he said.

He raised his shoulders and squared his elbows and took a few mincing steps across the room. He looked so funny—and yet so much like Imogen—that Katy couldn't help laughing.

The doctor sat down again and drew her close to him.

"You're an affectionate child, Katy," he said, "and I'm glad of it, but there is such a thing as throwing away one's affection. I didn't fancy that little girl at all yesterday. What makes you like her so much?"

"I didn't like her so much yesterday," Katy admitted reluctantly. "She's a lot nicer than that at school, sometimes."

"I'm glad to hear it," said her father. "What was that nonsense I heard her telling you about brigands?"

"It really hap—" began Katy. Then she caught her father's eye and bit her lip. "Well," she went on, laugh-

ing, "I suppose it didn't really happen. But it was ever so funny, even if it was all made up."

"Made-up things are all very well," her father said, "as long as people don't try to make you believe they are real. When they do that, it seems to me it comes too near the edge of falsehood to be very safe or pleasant. If I were you, I'd be a little shy of swearing undying friendship for Miss Clark. I think in two or three years from now she won't seem as nice to you as she does now. Give me a kiss, chick, and run away, for I must be off on my rounds."

Chapter Seven
Cousin Helen's Visit

It was an afternoon in July, and a little knot of school-girls were walking home together. As they neared Dr Carr's gate, one of them, Maria Fiske, gave an excited exclamation and pointed to a pretty bunch of flowers lying in the middle of the path.

"Look what somebody's dropped!" she cried. "I'm going to have it."

She stopped to pick it up, but just as her fingers touched the stems the flowers, as if bewitched, began to move. Maria made a grab. The flowers moved faster, and at last vanished under the hedge. There came a giggle from the other side.

"Katy, did you see that?" shrieked Maria. "Those flowers ran away from me!"

"Nonsense," said Katy, "it's those absurd children." Then, opening the gate, she called: "John! Dorry! Come out and show yourselves."

Nobody replied, and no one could be seen.

Katy bent down, reached under the hedge, and pulled out the flowers. She showed the girls a long length of black thread, tied to the stems.

"That's a favourite trick of Johnnie's," she said. "Here,

Maria, take them if you like. Though I don't think John's taste in bouquets is very good."

"Oh, thank you!" cried Maria.

"Isn't it lovely that the holidays are here!" said one of the bigger girls. "What are you all going to do? We're going to the sea-side."

All the group except Katy and Clover told where they were going to spend the summer holiday.

"What are you going to do, Katy?" someone asked.

"Oh, I don't know—play about and have fun," Katy replied, throwing her bag of books into the air and catching it again.

The other girls looked as if they were sorry for her, and Katy felt suddenly that her holiday wasn't going to be as pleasant as that of the rest.

"I wish father *would* take us somewhere," she said to Clover, as they walked up the path.

"He's too busy," said Clover, "but I wouldn't change him for anything."

"Neither would I," said Katy, her face brightening. "Oh, isn't it lovely to think there won't be any school tomorrow!"

They burst open the front door and raced upstairs crying, "Hurrah! no school for eight weeks!" Then they stopped short, for the upper hall was all in confusion. Sounds of beating and dusting came from the spare room. Tables and chairs were standing about, and a cot-bed, which seemed to be taking a walk all by itself,

had stopped short at the head of the stairs and barred the way.

Aunt Izzie came bustling out of the spare room. She looked very hot and flustered.

"Now, children," she said, "it's no use standing there. Go right downstairs, both of you, and don't come up this way again till after tea. I've as much as I can attend to till then."

"Just tell us what's going to happen, and we will," cried the children.

"Your Cousin Helen is coming to visit us," said Aunt Izzie curtly, and disappeared into the spare room once more.

This was news indeed. Katy and Clover ran downstairs in great excitement to talk it all over. Cousin Helen coming! It was as if a person out of one of their favourite books was coming to stay. None of the children had ever seen Cousin Helen. Philly said he was sure she hadn't any legs, because she never went away from home, but just lay on a sofa all the time. But the rest of them knew that this was because their cousin was ill. Their father went to visit her twice a year, and he liked to talk to the children about her, and tell them how sweet and patient she was.

It seemed a long time till the next afternoon, when Cousin Helen was expected. Aunt Izzie gave the children many orders about their behaviour. They were to do this and that, and not to do the other. Dorry, at last,

announced that he wished Cousin Helen would just stay at home if he'd got to do all *that.*

Five o'clock came. They all sat on the steps waiting for the carriage. At last it drove up. Father was on the box, and he waved for the children to stand back. Then he helped out a nice-looking woman, who, Aunt Izzie told them, was Cousin Helen's nurse. Then, very carefully, he lifted Cousin Helen from the carriage and brought her in his arms.

"Oh, there are the chicks!" said a cheerful and pleasant voice. "Do set me down somewhere, Uncle. I want to see them so much!"

So Dr Carr put Cousin Helen on the hall sofa, and called the children closer.

"So this is Katy," said the bright voice. "Why, what a tall Katy it is!"

Then she hugged them all round as if she loved them and wanted them all her life.

There was something in her face and manner which made the children at home with Cousin Helen. She had brown hair, which didn't curl, a brown skin, and bright eyes which laughed and danced when she spoke. Her face was thin, but except for that you wouldn't have guessed that she was sick.

By and by, father carried her upstairs. All the children wanted to go too, but he told them she was tired and must rest.

"Oh, do let me take up the tray," cried Katy at the

tea-table, as she watched Aunt Izzie getting ready Cousin Helen's supper. And such a nice supper! Cold chicken, and raspberries and cream, and a pretty pink-and-white china cup for her tea.

"No, indeed," said Aunt Izzie, " you might drop it."

But Katy's eyes begged so hard that Dr Carr said: "Yes, let her take it. I like to see the girls being useful."

So Katy took the tray and carried it carefully across the hall. There was a bowl of flowers on the table. She laid down the tray, and, picking out a rose, laid it beside the saucer of crimson raspberries. It looked very pretty.

"What are you stopping for?" Aunt Izzie called. "*Do* be careful, Katy."

"I'm almost up already," Katy called back, and sped upstairs as fast as she could go. Of course, it had to happen! She had just reached the door of Cousin Helen's room when she tripped. She caught at the door to save herself; the door flew open; and Katy, with the tray, cream, raspberries, rose and all, fell in a confused heap upon the carpet.

"I told you so," exclaimed Aunt Izzie from the bottom of the stairs.

Katy never forgot how kind Cousin Helen was. She was in bed, and a good deal startled by the crash. But, after one little jump, nothing could have been sweeter than the way in which she comforted poor Katy, and made so merry over the accident that even Aunt Izzie almost forgot to scold. The broken dishes were piled up

and the carpet made clean again, while Aunt Izzie prepared another tray just as nice as the first.

"Please let Katy bring it up!" pleaded Cousin Helen. "I'm sure she'll be careful this time. And Katy, I want another rose on the tray. That was your idea, wasn't it?"

Katy *was* careful and this time all went well. She sat watching Cousin Helen eat her supper with a warm, loving feeling at her heart. Cousin Helen hadn't much appetite, though she said that everything was delicious. Katy could see that she was very tired.

"Now," she said, when she had finished, "if you'll shake up this pillow, so, and move this other pillow a little, I think I'll settle myself to sleep. Thanks, that's just right. Why, Katy, dear, you're a born nurse! Now kiss me. Good night. Tomorrow we'll have a nice talk."

Katy went downstairs feeling very happy.

Next morning all the children were up early. They all wanted to see Cousin Helen at once, but she didn't wake till late. Katy went out into the garden to pick the prettiest flowers she could find to give to Cousin Helen the moment she should see her.

When Aunt Izzie let her go up, Cousin Helen was lying on the sofa all dressed for the day. She was white and tired, but her eyes and smile were as bright as ever. She was delighted with the flowers, which Katy presented rather shyly.

While they were talking together, they suddenly heard the queerest noise outside the door—a sort of snuffling

and snorting sound, as if a walrus or a sea-horse were promenading up and down in the hall. Katy opened the door. There were Johnnie and Dorry, very red in the face from flattening their noses against the keyhole, in a vain attempt to see if Cousin Helen were up and ready to receive company.

"Oh, let them come in!" she cried from her sofa.

So they came in, followed, before long, by Clover and Elsie. Then the fun began!

Cousin Helen could tell the most wonderful stories, and was full of ideas for games which could be played about her sofa. Aunt Izzie, dropping in about eleven o'clock, found them having such a good time, that almost before she knew it *she* was drawn into the game too. Nobody had ever heard of *that* before!

"What have you been doing to them, Helen?" asked Dr Carr, when he came home at noon, opened the door, and saw the merry circle around the sofa. "I must put a stop to this," he added. "Cousin Helen will be worn out. Run away, all of you, and don't come near this door again till the clock strikes four. Do you hear? Run, run! Shoo, shoo!"

The children scuttled away like a brood of fowls—all but Katy.

"Let me stay till the dinner-bell rings," she begged. "I'll be *so* quiet!"

"Yes, do let her!" said Cousin Helen.

So father said, "Yes."

Katy sat on the floor, holding Cousin Helen's hand, and listening to her talk with father. It interested her, though it was about things and people she did not know.

"How is Alex?" asked Dr Carr.

"Quite well now," replied Cousin Helen. "He was run down and tired in the spring, and we were a little anxious about him, but Emma got him away for a fortnight's holiday, and he came back all right."

"Do you see them often?"

"Almost every day. And little Helen comes every day, you know, for her lessons."

"Is she as pretty as she used to be?"

"Oh, yes—prettier, I think. Alex tries to make out that she looks a little as I used to, but that is a compliment so great that I can't believe it."

Dr Carr stooped and kissed Cousin Helen as if he could not help doing it. "My *dear* child," he said. That was all, but something in his tone made Katy curious.

"Father," she said, after dinner, "who is Alex that you and Cousin Helen were talking about?"

Dr Carr drew her on to his knee.

"I'll tell you about it, Katy," he said, "because you're old enough to see how beautiful it is, and wise enough, I hope, not to chatter or ask questions. Alex is the name of somebody, who, long ago, when Cousin Helen was well and strong, she loved, and expected to marry."

"Oh, why didn't she?" cried Katy.

"She met with a dreadful accident, and it was thought

for a long time that she would die. Then she grew slowly
better, and the doctors told her she might live a good
many years, but that she would have to lie on her sofa
always, and be helpless and a cripple.

"Alex felt this dreadfully when he heard it. He wanted
to marry her just the same, and be her nurse and take
care of her always, but she would not agree to that. She
broke the engagement, and told him that some day she
hoped he would love somebody else well enough to
marry her. So, after a good many years, he did, and
now he and his wife live next door to Cousin Helen
and are her dearest friends. Their little girl is named
Helen, after her. All their plans are talked over with
her, and there is nobody in the world they think so much
of."

There was a little silence.

"Doesn't it make Cousin Helen feel bad when she sees
them walking about and enjoying themselves, while she
can't move?" asked Katy.

"No," said Dr Carr, "it doesn't; because Cousin Helen
is half an angel already, and loves other people better
than herself. I'm very glad she could come here for once.
She's an example to us all, Katy."

"It must be *awful* to be ill," Katy thought, after her
father had gone. "Why, if I had to stay in bed a whole
week I should *die*. I know I should!"

That afternoon, when four o'clock came, all six children galloped upstairs to see Cousin Helen.

· "I think we'll tell stories this time," she said.

So they told stories. Cousin Helen's were the best of all. There was one about a robber which sent chills skating up and down their backs. They loved every moment of it.

It was no use, after this, for Aunt Izzie to make rules about when the children should go to see Cousin Helen. She might as well have ordered flies to keep away from the sugar-bowl. By hook or by crook, the children *would* get upstairs. Cousin Helen didn't seem to mind at all.

"We've only three or four days to be together," she said. "Let them come as much as they like. It won't hurt me a bit."

When the last evening came, and they went up after tea, Cousin Helen was opening a box which had just come by express delivery.

"It's a Good-bye Box," she said. "All of you must sit down in a row, and when I hide my hands behind me *so*, you must choose in turn which you will take."

So they all chose in turn and Cousin Helen, with the air of a wise fairy, brought out from behind her pillow something pretty for each one. Katy was given a beautiful little vase; next came a pocket-book for Clover; then a sweet little locket on a bit of velvet ribbon for Elsie, a box of dominoes for Dorry, and a book about robbers for Phil. Nobody was forgotten.

Next day came the sad parting. All the little ones stood at the gate to wave their handkerchiefs as the carriage

drove away. When it was quite out of sight, Katy rushed off to "weep a little weep", all by herself.

"Father said he wished we were all like Cousin Helen," she thought, as she wiped her eyes, "and I mean to try, though I don't suppose if I tried for a thousand years I should ever grow to be half so good. Dear me, if only Aunt Izzie was Cousin Helen, how easy it would be! Never mind! I'll think about her all the time, and I'll begin tomorrow."

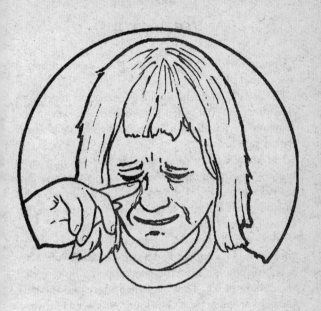

Chapter Eight

Tomorrow

"Tomorrow I'll begin," thought Katy, as she dropped asleep that night.

That was what she meant to do—to be an angel from that time on—but when she opened her eyes in the morning she felt all out of sorts and as peevish as a bear with a sore head.

You know what it's like to begin the day in a cross mood. All sorts of things seem to happen just to make us feel worse. Well, the very first thing Katy did this morning was to break her precious vase, the one that Cousin Helen had given her.

It was standing on the bureau with a little cluster of roses in it. The bureau had a swing-glass. While Katy was brushing her hair, the glass tipped a little so that she could not see. That made her angry and she gave the glass a violent push. The lower part swung forward, there was a smash, and the first thing Katy knew the roses lay scattered all over the floor, and Cousin Helen's pretty present was ruined.

Katy just sat down on the carpet and cried as hard as she knew how. Aunt Izzie heard her, and came in.

"I'm very sorry," she said, picking up the broken glass,

"but you are so careless, Katy. Now, get up and dress yourself. You'll be late for breakfast."

Katy ate her breakfast in a sulky silence.

"What are you all going to do today?" asked Dr Carr, hoping to give things a more cheerful turn.

"Swing!" cried Johnnie and Dorry together. "Alexander's put up a new one in the woodshed."

"No, you're not," said Aunt Izzie firmly. "The swing is not to be used until tomorrow. Remember that, children. Not till tomorrow. And not then, unless I say you may."

This was unwise of Aunt Izzie. She would have done better to have explained further. The truth was that Alexander, in putting up the swing, had cracked one of the staples which fastened it to the roof. He meant to get a new one in the course of the day, and, meantime, he had cautioned Aunt Izzie to let no one use the swing, because it really was not safe. If she had told this to the children, all would have been well; but Aunt Izzie believed that young people should obey their elders without explanation.

Johnnie and Dorry pouted when they heard this order.

"I don't care," said Elsie, "because I'm going to be very busy. I've got to write a letter to Cousin Helen about somefing." (Elsie never could quite pronounce the *th*.)

"What?" asked Clover.

Elsie wagged her head mysteriously.

"Oh, somefing!" she answered. "It's a secret I've got with Cousin Helen. She said you musn't know about it."

"I don't believe you," said Katy, crossly. "She wouldn't tell secrets to a silly little girl like you."

"Yes, she would, too," retorted Elsie angrily. "So there, Katy Carr!"

"Stop arguing," Aunt Izzie ordered. "Katy, your top drawer is all out of order. Go upstairs at once and straighten it, before you do anything else."

Katy went slowly upstairs. The day seemed too warm. Her head ached a little, and her eyes smarted from crying so much. Everything seemed dull and hateful. She said to herself that Aunt Izzie was very unkind to make her work in holiday time, and she pulled the top drawer open with a disgusted groan.

It took her a long time to straighten the things in it. All sorts of things were mixed up together, as if somebody had put in a long stick and stirred them well up. There were books and paint-boxes and bits of scribbled paper and lead pencils and brushes. Stocking-legs had come unrolled and twisted themselves about pocket handkerchiefs, and ends of ribbon, and linen collars.

Katy dared not stop till she had it all neatly sorted out. By the time it was finished she was very tired and irritable. Going downstairs, she met Elsie coming up with a slate in her hand, which, as soon as she saw Katy, she put behind her.

"You mustn't look," she said. "It's my letter to Cousin Helen. It's all written, and I'm going to the post-office. See—there's a stamp on it."

She showed a corner of the slate. Sure enough, there was a stamp stuck on the frame.

"You silly little goose!" said Katy, impatiently. "You can't send *that* by post. Here, give me the slate. I'll copy what you've written on paper, and Father will give you an envelope."

"No, no," cried Elsie, struggling, "you mustn't! You'll see what I've written, and Cousin Helen said I wasn't to tell. Let go my slate or I'll tell Cousin Helen what a mean girl you are!"

"There, then, take your old slate!" said Katy, and gave her sister a vindictive push.

Elsie slipped, screamed, caught at the banisters, missed them, and, rolling over and over, fell with a thump on the hall floor.

It wasn't much of a fall, only half a dozen steps, but the bump was a hard one, and Elsie roared as if she had been half-killed. Aunt Izzie came running.

"Katy—pushed—me," sobbed Elsie. "She wanted me to tell her my secret, and I wouldn't. She's a bad, naughty girl!"

"Katy, you should be ashamed of yourself," cried Aunt Izzie, "treating your poor little sister like that! There, there, Elsie! Don't cry any more, dear. Come upstairs with me...."

They went upstairs. Katy, left below, felt very miserable: repentant, defiant, discontented, and sulky all at once.

"I don't care!" she murmured, choking back her tears. "Elsie is a real cry-baby, anyway. And Aunt Izzie always takes her part. Just because I told the little silly not to go and send a great heavy slate to the post-office!"

She went out by the side-door into the yard. As she passed the shed, the new swing caught her eye.

"It's just like Aunt Izzie," she thought, "to order the children not to swing until she gives them leave. I suppose she thinks it's too hot, or something. *I* shan't mind her, anyhow."

She seated herself in the swing. It was a first-rate one, with a broad seat and thick new ropes. The wood-shed itself was a big place with a very high roof. There was not much wood left in it just now, and the little there was was piled neatly about the sides of the shed, so as to leave plenty of room.

Swinging to and fro like the pendulum of a great clock, Katy gradually rose higher and higher. Now she was at the top of the high arched door. Then she could almost touch the cross-beam above it, and through the small square window could see pigeons sitting pluming themselves on the eaves of the barn, and white clouds blowing over the blue sky.

Never had she swung so high before. It was like flying,

she thought, as she bent and curved more strongly in the seat, trying to send herself higher yet, and to graze the roof with her toes.

Suddenly, at the very highest point of the sweep, there came a sharp noise of cracking. The swing gave a violent twist, spun half round, and tossed Katy into the air. She clutched at the rope—felt it dragged from her grasp—then, down-down-down she fell.

Something struck her a sharp blow. Then all grew dark, and she knew no more.

Chapter Nine
A Hard Blow

When she opened her eyes she was lying on the sofa in the dining-room. Clover was kneeling beside her with a pale, scared face, and Aunt Izzie was dropping something cold and wet on to her forehead.

"What's the matter?" asked Katy, faintly.

"Oh, she's alive—she's alive!" cried Clover, and she put her arms round Katy's neck and burst into tears.

"Hush, dear!" Aunt Izzie's voice sounded unusually gentle. "You've had a tumble, Katy. Don't you remember?"

"A tumble? Oh, yes—out of the swing!" said Katy, as it all came slowly back to her. "Did the rope break? I can't remember about it."

"No, Katy, not the rope. The staples drew away from the roof. One was cracked and not safe. Don't you remember my telling you not to swing today? Did you forget?"

"No Aunt Izzie I didn't forget. I—" but here Katy broke down. She closed her eyes, and big tears rolled from under the lids.

"Don't cry," whispered Clover, still sobbing herself, "please don't. Aunt Izzie won't scold you."

However, Katy was too weak and shaken not to cry.

"I think I'd like to go upstairs and lie on the bed," she said.

But when she tried to get off the sofa, everything swam before her, and she fell back again on the pillow.

She was frightened.

"I can't stand up," she gasped.

Aunt Izzie looked very worried.

"I'm afraid you've given yourself a sprain somewhere," she said. "You'd better lie still a while, dear. Ah, here's the doctor, thank goodness!"

She went forward to meet him. It wasn't Katy's father, but Dr Alsop, who lived quite near them.

"I'm so glad you're here," Aunt Izzie said. "My brother has gone out of town and won't be back till tomorrow. One of the girls has had a bad fall."

Dr Alsop sat down beside the sofa and counted Katy's pulse. Then he began feeling all over her.

"Can you move this leg?" he asked.

Katy gave a feeble kick.

"And this?"

The kick was a good deal more feeble.

"Did that hurt you?" asked Dr Alsop, seeing the look of pain on her face.

"Yes, a little," replied Katy, trying hard not to cry.

"In your back, eh? Was the pain high up or low down?"

He punched Katy's spine for some minutes, making her wriggle and squirm uneasily.

"I'm afraid she's done some mischief," he said at last, "but it's impossible to tell exactly what. It may be only a twist, or a slight sprain," he added, seeing a look of terror on Katy's face. "You'd better get her upstairs and undress her as soon as you can, Miss Carr. I'll leave a prescription for something she can be rubbed with."

He took out a little book and began to write.

"Oh, must I go to bed?" asked Katy. "How long will I have to stay there?"

"That depends on how fast you get well," replied the doctor. "Not long, I hope. Perhaps only a few days."

Katy's face fell.

"A few days!" she gasped.

The idea filled her with despair.

After the doctor had gone, Aunt Izzie called in Alexander, and between them they lifted Katy and carried her slowly upstairs. It was not easy, for the movement hurt her, and the sense of being helpless hurt her most of all. She couldn't help crying after she was undressed and put into bed. It all seemed so dreadful and strange. If only her father were here, she thought. Dr Carr had gone into the country to see somebody who was very sick, and he couldn't possibly be back until the next morning.

It seemed such a long, long afternoon. Aunt Izzie sent up some dinner, but Katy couldn't eat. Her lips were parched and her head ached violently. The sun began to pour in, the room grew too warm. Flies buzzed in

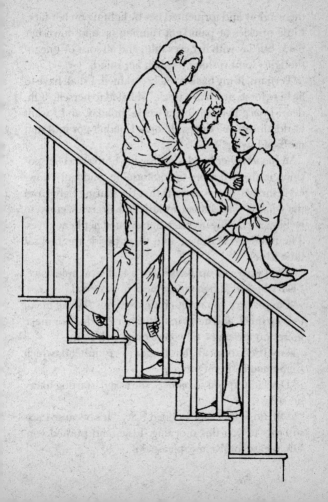

the window and tormented her by lighting on her face.
Little prickles of pain kept running up and down her
back. She lay with her eyes shut, and all sorts of uneasy
thoughts went rushing through her mind.

"Perhaps, if my back is really sprained, I shall have to
lie here for as much as a week," she said to herself. "Oh,
dear! I *can't*! I've only eight weeks' holiday, and I want
to do all sorts of things. If only I hadn't got into that
nasty old swing!"

All the time her head was growing hotter and her po-
sition in the bed more uncomfortable. Suddenly, however, she became conscious that the glaring light from
the window was shaded and that the breeze seemed to
be blowing freshly over her. She opened her heavy eyes.
The blinds were drawn, and there beside the bed sat
little Elsie.

"Did I wake you up, Katy?" she asked, in a timid voice.

Katy looked at her, amazement in her eyes.

"I'm so sorry you're ill," Elsie went on. "We all mean
to keep quiet, and never bang the nursery door, or make
noises on the stairs, till you're quite well again."

Katy tried to speak, but began to cry instead, which
frightened Elsie very much.

"Does it hurt you so badly?" she asked, starting to cry
herself.

"Oh, no, it isn't *that*," sobbed Katy. "It's because I was
so cross to you this morning, Elsie, and pushed you.
Oh, please forgive me, please do!"

She held out her arms. Elsie ran right into them, and the big sister and the little gave each other a hug which seemed to bring their hearts closer together than they had ever been before.

All the rest of the afternoon Elsie sat beside the bed with a palm-leaf fan, keeping off the flies and chasing away the other children when they peeped in at the door.

"I'll be so good to her when I get well," thought Katy, tossing uneasily to and fro.

Aunt Izzie slept in her room that night. Katy was feverish. When morning came, and Dr Carr returned, he found her in a good deal of pain, hot and restless, with wide-open, anxious eyes.

"Father!" she cried, as soon as she saw him, "must I lie here for a whole week?"

"My darling, I'm afraid you must," replied her father, who was looking very grave and worried.

"Oh, dear!" sobbed Katy, "however will I bear it?"

Chapter Ten
Dismal Days

If anybody had told Katy, that first afternoon, that at
the end of a week she would still be in bed, in pain, and
with no time fixed for getting up, I think it would almost have killed her. She was so restless and eager, that
to lie still seemed one of the hardest things in the world.
But to lie still and have her back ache all the time was
worse yet.

Day after day she asked her father, with quivering lips:
"May I get up this morning?"

Always he shook his head, and then her lips quivered
and the tears flowed. If, however, she tried to get up, it
hurt her so much that in spite of herself she was glad to
sink back on to the soft pillows and mattress.

Then there came a time when she didn't ever ask to
get up. A time when sharp, dreadful pain took hold of
her. When days and nights got all mixed up, and Aunt
Izzie never seemed to go to bed. A time when her father was often in her room. When other doctors came
and stood over her, and punched and felt her back and
talked to each other in low whispers. Then all these
things would slip away again and she would drop off
into a dark place where there was nothing but pain,

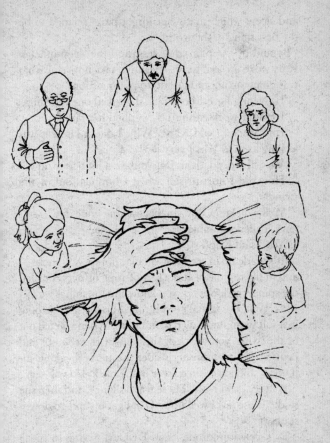

and sleep, which made her forget pain, seemed to be the best thing in the world.

By and by the pain grew less, and the sleep quieter. Katy woke up, as it were—began to take notice of what was going on about her and to put questions.

"How long have I been ill?" she asked one morning.

"It is four weeks yesterday," replied her father.

"Four weeks!" said Katy. "Why, I didn't know it was as long as that. Was I very ill?"

"Very ill indeed, dear. But you are a lot better now."

"How did I hurt myself when I tumbled out of the swing?"

"Well, you know that you have a long bone down your back, called the spine?"

"Yes," said Katy.

"It's made up of a row of smaller bones—or knobs—and in the middle of it is a sort of rope of nerves called the spinal cord. Nerves, you know, are the things we feel with. Well, this spinal cord is rolled up for safe-keeping in a soft wrapping called membrane. When you fell out of the swing, you struck against one of these knobs and bruised the membrane inside; the nerve became inflamed, and gave you a fever in the back. Do you see?"

"A little," said Katy. There was a silence, and then she said: "Is the fever well now? Can I get up and go downstairs yet?"

"Not yet, I'm afraid," said Dr Carr, trying to speak cheerfully.

Katy didn't ask any more questions then. Another week passed, and another. The pain was almost gone. It only came back now and then for a few minutes. She could sleep now, and eat, and be raised in bed without feeling giddy; but still she was not able to walk, or even stand alone.

"My legs feel so strange ," she said one morning. "Why is that? Won't they feel stronger soon?"

"Not soon," answered Dr Carr quietly. "I'm afraid, my darling, that you must make up your mind to stay in bed a long time."

Katy looked frightened.

"How long?" she asked. "Another month?"

"I can't tell you exactly how long. The doctors think, as I do, that the injury to your spine is one that you will outgrow by and by, because you are so young and strong. That may take a good while to do. It may be that you will have to lie here for months, or even longer. The only cure for such a hurt is time and patience. It's hard, darling, I know,"—for Katy began to sob wildly—"but you have hope to help you along. Think of poor Cousin Helen bearing all these years without even the hope of getting better."

Years afterwards, Katy told somebody that the six longest weeks of her life were those which followed this talk with her father. Now that she knew there was no chance of her getting well at once, the days dragged dreadfully. Each seemed duller and dismaller than the one before.

She lost heart about herself and took no interest in anything. She didn't want to read, or sew. Nothing amused her. Clover and Cecy would come to sit with her, but hearing them tell about their play, and the things they had been doing, made her cry so miserably that Aunt Izzie wouldn't let them come too often. They were very sorry for Katy, but the room was so gloomy, and Katy so cross, that they didn't much mind not being allowed to see her. In those days Katy made Aunt Izzie keep the blinds shut tight, and she lay in the dark, thinking how miserable she was, and how wretched all the rest of her life was going to be.

And then something happened to break into this dreadful state of affairs. Cousin Helen came back, just for one day. This time Katy was not on the steps to welcome her, but Dr Carr brought her up in his arms and sat her in a big chair beside the bed.

"How dark it is in here!" said Cousin Helen, after they had kissed and talked for a minute or two. "I can't see your face at all. Would it hurt your eyes to have a little more light?"

"Oh, no," Katy answered, "only—I hate to have the sun come in. It makes me feel worse, somehow."

"Push the blinds open a little bit, then, Clover," said Cousin Helen.

Clover did so.

"Now I can see you," Cousin Helen said.

It was a sad-looking child she saw lying before her.

Katy's face had grown thin, and her eyes had red circles about them from continual crying. Her hair had been brushed twice that morning by Aunt Izzie, but Katy had run her fingers impatiently through it till it stood out above her head like a bush. She wore a calico dressing gown that was ugly in pattern; and the room, for all its tidiness, had a dismal look, with the chairs set up against the wall, and a row of medicine bottles on the mantelpiece.

"Isn't it horrid?" Katy sighed. "Everything's horrid! But I don't mind so much now that you've come. Oh, Cousin Helen, I've had such a *dreadful* time!"

"I know," said her cousin pityingly. "I've heard all about it. It's a hard trial, my poor darling."

"But how do *you* do it?" cried Katy. "How do you manage to be so sweet and beautiful and patient, when you're feeling badly all the time, and can't do anything, or walk, or stand..." her voice was lost in sobs.

Cousin Helen didn't say anything for a little while. She just sat and stroked Katy's hand. Yet, in some odd way, Katy felt that Cousin Helen had done her good already. She felt brighter and less listless than for days.

"I'll tell you a story if you like," said Cousin Helen at last. "It's about a girl I once knew. She was quite young, and strong and active. She liked to run, and climb, and ride, and do all sorts of jolly things. One day something happened—an accident—and they told her that all the rest of her life she had got to lie on her back and suffer

pain, and never walk any more, or do any of the things she enjoyed most of all."

"Just like you and me!" whispered Katy, squeezing Cousin Helen's hand.

"Something like me; but not so much like you, because we hope that *you* are going to get well one of these days. The girl didn't mind it so much when they first told her, for she was so ill that she felt sure she would die. Then she grew better, and began to think of the long life which lay before her, which was worse than ever the pain had been. She was so wretched that she didn't care what became of anything, or how anything looked. Her room got into a dreadful state. It was full of dust and confusion, and dirty spoons and bottles of medicine. She kept the blinds shut, and let her hair tangle any way, and altogether she was a very sorry sight indeed.

"Now, this girl had a dear old father, who used to come every day and sit beside her bed. One morning he said to her:

"'My dear, I'm afraid you've got to live in this room for a very long time. Now, here's something I want you to do for my sake.'

"'What's that?' she asked, surprised to hear that there was anything left which she could do for anybody.

"'I want you to turn out all these medicine bottles, and make your room pleasant and pretty for *me* to come and sit in. You see, I shall spend a good deal of *my* time

here! I don't like dust and darkness. I like to see flowers on the table, and sunshine in at the window. Will you do this to please me?'

"'Yes,' said the girl, but she gave a sigh, and I'm afraid that she felt it was all going to be the most dreadful trouble.

"'There's another thing,' her father went on. 'I want you to look pretty. A sick person ought to be as fresh and dainty as a rose. Can't nightdresses and dressing gowns be trimmed and made becoming just as much as dresses? Do, to please me, send for something pretty and let me see you looking nice again. I can't bear to have my Helen turn into a slattern!'"

Katy's eyes widened.

"Helen!" she exclaimed. "Was it you?"

"Yes," said her cousin, smiling. "It was—though I didn't mean to let the name slip out so soon. Anyway, after my father had gone, I sent for a looking-glass. Such a sight I saw, Katy! My hair was like a mouse's nest, and I had frowned so much that my forehead was all criss-crossed with lines of pain till it looked like an old woman's."

Katy stared at her cousin's smooth brow and glossy hair.

"I can't believe it," she said. "Your hair could never be rough."

"Yes it was—a lot worse than yours looks now. But that peep in the glass did me good. I began to think

how selfishly I was behaving, and to want to do better. After that, when the pain came on, I used to lie and keep my forehead smooth with my fingers, and try not to let my face show what I was going through. So by and by the wrinkles went away, and though I am a good deal older now, they have never come back.

"It was a great deal of trouble at first to have to think and plan to keep my room and myself looking nice, but after a while it grew to be a habit, and then it became easy. And the pleasure it gave my father paid for it all. He had been proud of his healthy daughter, but I think she was never such a comfort to him as his sick one, lying there in her bed. My room, after that, was his favourite sitting-place, and he spent so much time there that now the room and everything in it makes me think of him."

There were tears in Cousin Helen's eyes as she stopped speaking. Katy looked bright and eager.

"Do you really think I could do the same?" she asked.

"Do what? Comb your hair?"

Cousin Helen was smiling again.

"Oh, no! Be nice and sweet and patient, and a comfort to people. You know what I mean."

"I'm sure you can, if you try."

"What would you do first?" asked Katy.

"Well, first of all I'd open the blinds and make the room look a little less dismal. Are you taking all those medicines in the bottles now?"

"No, only that big one with the blue label."

"Then you might ask Aunt Izzie to take away the others. And I'd get Clover to pick a bunch of fresh flowers every day for your table. By the way, I don't see the little vase I gave you."

"No, it got broken the day I fell out of the swing," said Katy sorrowfully.

"Never mind, I'll see you get another. Then, after the room is made pleasant, I'd have all my lesson-books fetched up if I were you, and I'd study for a couple of hours every morning. That will stop you getting too far behind."

"Oh!" cried Katy, and made a wry face.

Her cousin smiled.

"I know," she said, "it sounds like dull work, learning geography and doing sums up here by yourself, but I think if you make a start you'll be glad by and by. You won't lose so much ground, you see."

"Well," said Katy, rather doubtfully, "I'll try. Is there anything else, Cousin Helen?"

Just then the door creaked, and Elsie timidly put her head into the room.

"Oh, Elsie, run away!" cried Katy. "Cousin Helen and I are talking. Don't come just now."

Elsie's face fell, and she looked disappointed. She said nothing, however, but shut the door and stole away.

Cousin Helen watched this little scene without speaking. For a few minutes after Elsie had gone, she seemed lost in thought.

"Katy," she said at last, "you were saying just now that one of the things you were sorry about was that while you were ill you could be of no use to the children. Do you know, I don't think you have that reason for being sorry."

"Why not?" said Katy, astonished.

"Because you *can* be of use. It seems to me that you have more of a chance with the children now, than you ever could have had when you were well, the way you used to fly about. You might do almost anything you liked with them."

"I can't think what you mean," said Katy sadly. "Why, half the time I don't even know where they are, or what they are doing. And I can't get up and go after them, you know."

"But can't you make your room such a delightful place that they will want to come to you? Don't you see, a sick person has one splendid chance—she is always on hand. Everybody who wants her knows just where to go. If people love her, she gets to be the heart of a house.

"If you can make the little ones feel that your room is the one place above all others to come to when they are tired, or happy, or sad, or sorry about anything, and that the Katy who lives there is sure to be glad to see them—the battle is won. But I didn't mean to preach a sermon. I'm afraid you're tired."

"No, I'm not a bit," said Katy. "You can't think how much better I feel. Oh, Cousin Helen, I *will* try!"

"It won't be easy," replied her cousin. "There'll be days when your head aches and you feel cross and don't want to think of anyone but yourself. There'll be other days when Clover and the rest will come in, as Elsie did just now, and you'll be doing something else, and feel as if their coming was an awful bother. But you must remember that every time you forget, and are impatient or selfish, you'll chill them and drive them further away. They're loving little things, and are so sorry for you now, that nothing you do makes them angry. By and by they'll get used to having you sick, and if you haven't won them as friends they'll grow away from you as they get older."

Just then Dr Carr came in.

"I think the big invalid and the little invalid have talked long enough," he said. "Cousin Helen looks tired."

For a minute Katy felt just like crying. She didn't want Cousin Helen to go, but she choked back the tears, and managed to give a faint, watery smile as her father looked at her.

That night Katy had a strange dream. She thought she was trying to study a lesson out of a book which wouldn't quite come open. She could see just a little bit of what was inside, but it was in a language she could not understand. She tried in vain: not a word could she read; and yet, for all that, it looked so interesting that she longed to go on.

"Oh, if somebody would only help me!" she cried impatiently.

Suddenly a hand came over her shoulder and took
hold of the book. It opened at once and showed the
whole page. Then the forefinger of the hand began to
point to line after line, and as it moved the words became plain and Katy could read them easily.

She looked up. There, stooping over her, was a great
beautiful Face. The eyes met hers. The lips smiled.

"Why didn't you ask me to help before?" said a Voice.

"Why, it is *You*!" cried Katy.

She must have spoken in her sleep, for Aunt Izzie half
woke up and said:

"What is it? Do you want anything?"

The dream broke and Katy roused, to find herself in
bed, with the first sunbeams straggling in at the window, and Aunt Izzie raised on her elbow, looking at her
with a sort of sleepy wonder.

Chapter Eleven
The Chair

After Cousin Helen's visit, things were very different for Katy. Within a few weeks she had made her room a very pleasant place, and one where the children loved to gather. Everything was neat and orderly, the air was always sweet with the scent of flowers, and the Katy who lay in bed was a very different-looking Katy from the forlorn girl of the last chapter.

Not that she grew perfect all at once. None of us does that, even in books. But it counts for a lot to be started on the right path, and Katy's feet were on it now....

There were bad days, of course, when everything seemed hard, and she herself was cross and fretful, and drove the children out of her room. These days cost Katy many bitter tears. But after them she would pick herself up, and try again, and harder.

Cousin Helen was a great comfort all this time. She never forgot Katy. Nearly every week some little thing came from her. Sometimes it was just a pencil note, written from her sofa. Sometimes it was an interesting book, or a new magazine, or some pretty little thing for the room. The crimson dressing gown which Katy often wore was one of her presents—and there were many

other things. All the room seemed, to Katy, to be full of
Cousin Helen and her kindness.

Christmas came in a flurry of snow. All the stockings
were hung up in Katy's room, so that she should have a
share in all the fun and games, and it was there that the
presents were handed out to the family.

For Katy, there were two presents that meant more to
her than all the others. One of them was a chair, a very
large and curious one, with a long cushioned back, that
ended in a footstool.

"That's *my* present," said Dr Carr. "See, it tips back
so as to be just like a bed. Very soon now, my darling,
you can lie on it, in the window, where you can watch
the children play."

"And see what's tied to the arm of the chair," put in
Elsie excitedly.

It was a little silver bell, with "Katy" engraved on the
handle.

"Cousin Helen sent it. It's for you to ring when you
want anybody to come," Elsie explained.

"How perfectly lovely everybody is!" said Katy, with
tears of gratitude in her eyes.

That was a wonderful Christmas. The children said
that it was the nicest they had ever had. And though
Katy couldn't quite say that, she enjoyed it too, and
was very happy.

It was several weeks before she was able to use the
chair, but when once she got used to it, it proved very

comfortable. Aunt Izzie would dress her in the morning, tip the chair back till it was on a level with the bed, and then, very gently and gradually, draw her over on to it. Wheeling across the room was always painful, but sitting in the window and looking out at the clouds, the people going by, and the children playing in the snow, was delightful.

As the months rolled by, Katy's chair became a great comfort to her. She could sit up in it and roll herself across the room to her cupboards and bureau-drawers, and help herself to what she wanted without troubling anybody.

Autumn came and went, and it was winter once more. This second winter was harder than the first. It is often so with sick people. There is a sort of excitement in being ill which helps along just at the beginning. Then, as months go on, and everything grows an old story, and one day follows another day, all just alike, and all tiresome, courage is apt to flag and spirits to grow dull. Spring seemed a long, long way off whenever Katy thought about it.

"I wish something would happen," she often said to herself.

Something was about to happen, but she little guessed what it was going to be.

"Katy," said Clover, coming in one day in November, "I'll have to look after you today. Aunt Izzie has got *such* a headache."

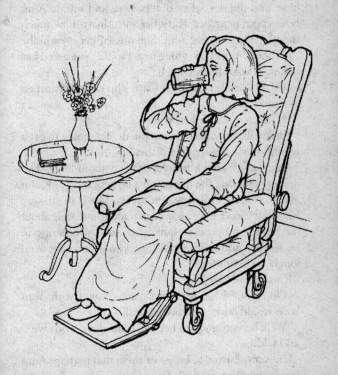

"How very strange!" thought Katy, when Clover was gone. "I never knew Aunt Izzie to have a headache before."

It seemed stranger yet, when the next day, and the next, and the next after that passed, and still no Aunt Izzie came near her. Katy began to learn how much she had relied on her aunt. She missed her dreadfully.

"When *is* Aunt Izzie going to get well ?" she asked her father. "I want her so much."

"We all want her," said Dr Carr, who looked disturbed and anxious.

"Is she very ill?" asked Katy.

"Pretty ill, I'm afraid," he replied. "I'm going to get a regular nurse to take care of her."

Aunt Izzie's attack proved to be typhoid fever. The doctors said that the house must be kept quiet, so John and Dorry and Phil were sent over to Mrs Hall's to stay. Elsie and Clover were allowed to remain, and stole about the house on tiptoe, as quietly as mice, whispering to each other, and waiting on Katy, who would have been lonely without them.

It was a sad time.

"Oh, dear," Elsie kept on saying, "how I wish Aunt Izzie would hurry up and get well!"

"We'll be very good to her when she does, won't we?" said Clover.

It never occurred to either of them that perhaps Aunt Izzie might not get well. Even Katy did not wholly re-

alize the danger. So it came like a sudden and violent
shock to her, when, one morning on waking up, she
found Clover and Elsie crying quietly beside the bed.

Aunt Izzie had died in the night.

For the first time, the three girls, sobbing in each other's arms, realized what a good friend Aunt Izzie had
been to them. Her worrying ways were all forgotten now.
They could only remember the many things she had done
for them since they were little children. How they wished
that they had never teased her, never said sharp words
about her to each other! But it was no use to wish.

"What shall we do without Aunt Izzie?" thought Katy,
as she cried herself to sleep that night.

For several days she saw almost nothing of her father.
Then, one evening after tea, he came upstairs to sit a
while in Katy's room. He looked very tired, and it
seemed to Katy that his face had grown older of late.

"I've been thinking how we are to manage about the
housekeeping," said Dr Carr. "Of course we shall have
to get somebody to come and take charge. But it isn't
easy to find just the right person. Do you think you can
get on as you are for a few days?"

"Oh!" cried Katy, in dismay, "must we have anybody?"

"What else can we do?" asked her father. "Clover is
much too young for a housekeeper. Besides, she's at
school all day."

An idea flashed into Katy's head. Her eyes suddenly
sparkled.

"Father," she said, "I wish you'd let *me* try. Really and truly, I think I could manage."

"But how?" asked Dr Carr, much surprised. "If you were well and strong perhaps—but even then you'd be pretty young for such a charge, Katy."

"I shall be fourteen in two weeks," said Katy, "and I can't go to school, remember. I'll tell you my plan. Debby and Bridget have cooked and cleaned up for so long, that they know all Aunt Izzie's ways, and they're so good that all they want is to be told a little now and then. Now, why couldn't they come up to me when anything is wanted—just as well as have me go down to them. Do let me try! It will be nice to have something to think about as I sit up here alone. I'm sure it will make me happier. Please say 'Yes', Father, please do!"

To her joy, her father agreed to let her try.

"Poor child, anything to take her thoughts off herself!" he muttered, as he walked downstairs. "She'll be glad enough to give the thing up by the end of a month."

But he was mistaken. At the end of a month Katy was eager to go on.

It was not such hard work as it sounds. Katy had plenty of quiet thinking-time for one thing. She could plan out her hours and keep to the plan. That is a great help to a housekeeper.

Then Aunt Izzie's regular, punctual ways were so well understood by the servants, that the house seemed almost to keep itself. As Katy had said, all Debby

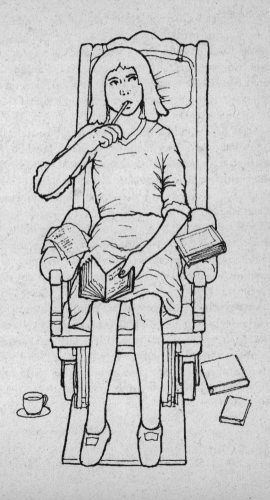

and Bridget needed was a little "telling" now and then.

As soon as breakfast was over, and the dishes were washed and put away, Debby would tie on a clean apron, and come upstairs for orders. At first Katy thought this great fun, but after ordering a dinner a good many times, it began to grow tiresome. It seemed impossible to think of enough to make a variety of meals.

Then Katy would send for every recipe-book in the house, and pore over them by the hour. Poor Debby learned to dread these books. She would stand by the door with her pleasant red face drawn up into a pucker, while Katy worked out how to make some highly unusual dish.

Dr Carr had to eat a great many strange things in those days. He didn't mind, however, and as for the children, they enjoyed it. Dinner-time became quite exciting, when nobody could tell exactly what any dish on the table was made of.

After a while Katy grew wiser. Month by month she learned how to manage a little better, and a little better still. Matters went on more smoothly. Her cares ceased to fret her. Nothing more was said about "somebody else", and Katy, sitting upstairs in her big chair, held the threads of the house firmly in her hands.

Chapter Twelve

At Last

It was a pleasant morning in early June. A warm wind was rustling the trees, which were thickly covered with half-opened leaves that looked like fountains of green spray thrown high into the air.

Clover and Elsie were busy downstairs, when they were startled by the sound of Katy's bell ringing in a sudden and agitated manner. Both ran upstairs two at a time to see what was wanted.

Katy sat bolt upright in her chair. She looked very flushed and excited.

"Girls!" she exclaimed. "What do you think? I stood up!"

"What!" cried Clover and Elsie.

"I really did! I stood up on my feet—by myself!"

The others stared at her, too astonished to speak, so Katy went on explaining.

"It was all at once, you see. Suddenly I had the feeling that if I tried I could, and almost before I thought, I *did* try, and there I was, up and out of the chair. Only I kept hold of the arm all the time! I don't know how I got back, I was so frightened. Oh, girls!"—and Katy buried her face in her hands.

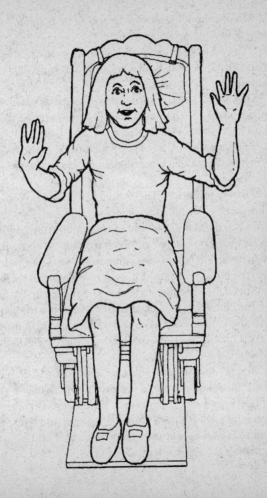

"Do you think I shall ever be able to do it again?" she asked, looking up with wet eyes.

"Why, of course you will!" said Clover; while Elsie danced about, crying out anxiously: "Be careful! Do be careful!"

Katy tried, but the spring was gone. She could not move out of the chair at all. She began to wonder if she had dreamed the whole thing.

Next day, when Clover happened to be in the room, she heard a sudden cry, and turned. There stood Katy on her feet!

"Dorry, Johnnie, Elsie!" shrieked Clover, rushing downstairs. "Come at once—come and see!"

Dr Carr was out, but all the rest came crowding up. Katy found no trouble in "doing it again". It seemed as if her will had been asleep; and, now that it had waked up, the limbs recognized its orders and obeyed them.

When Dr Carr came in, he was as much excited as any of the children. He walked round and round the chair, questioning Katy and making her stand up and sit down.

"Am I really going to get well?" she asked, almost in a whisper.

"Yes, my love, I think you are," replied Dr Carr, seizing Phil and giving him a toss into the air. None of the children had ever before seen him so excited. Pretty soon, noticing Katy's burning cheeks and eyes, he calmed himself, sent the others away, and sat down to quiet her with gentle words.

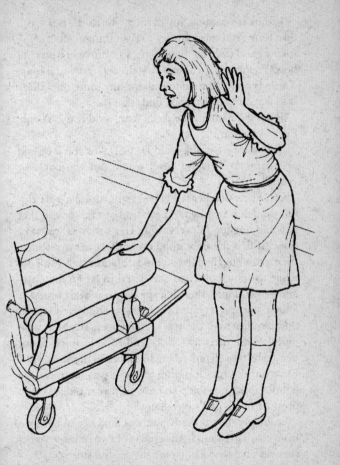

"I think it's coming, my darling," he said, "but it will take time. You must not try to rush things. After being such a good child all these years, I'm sure you won't fail now. You must be content to gain very little at a time. There is no royal road to walking any more than there is to learning. Every baby finds that out."

"It doesn't matter if it takes a year," said Katy, "if only I get well at last."

"You *must* be careful," said Dr Carr, "or you'll be laid up again. A course of fever would put you back for years."

Katy knew that her father was right, and she *was* careful, though it was by no means easy to be so with that new life tingling in every limb. Her progress was very slow. At first she only stood on her feet a few seconds, then a minute, then five minutes, holding tightly all the while to the chair. Next she dared to let go the chair and stand alone. After that she began to walk a step at a time, pushing a chair before her, as children do when they are learning the use of their feet. It was a little pitiful to see the way Clover and Elsie hovered about her as she moved unsteadily, like anxious mammas. But Katy did not find it pitiful; to her it was the most delightful thing possible. No baby of a year old was ever prouder of his first steps than she.

Gradually she grew adventurous, and began to move from room to room. In the course of two or three weeks she was able to walk all over the second storey.

This was a great enjoyment. It was like reading an interesting book to see all the new things, and the little changes that had been made in the house.

By the end of August she had grown so strong that she began to talk about going downstairs. But her father said, "Wait."

"It will tire you much more than walking about on a level," he explained. "You had better put it off a little while—till you are quite sure of your feet."

"I think so too," said Clover, "and besides, I want to have the house all put in order and made nice, before your sharp eyes see it, Mrs Housekeeper. Oh, I'll tell you! You fix a day to come down, Katy, and we'll all be ready for you, and have a 'celebration party' among ourselves. That would be just lovely! How soon may she, Father?"

"Well, in ten days, I should say, it might be safe."

"Ten days! That would bring it to the seventh of September," said Katy. "If I may, I'll come down for the first time on the eighth. That was mother's birthday, you know," she added in a lower voice.

So it was settled that the celebration would take place on the eighth.

Clover seemed to be very busy all the rest of that week. And Katy got the idea that some sort of secret surprise was being planned. The other children had evidently been warned to say nothing; for once or twice Philly broke out with, "Oh, Katy!" and then hushed himself up, say-

ing, "I almost forgot!" Katy grew very curious, but was wise enough not to spoil the fun by asking any questions.

At last there was just one day to go before the great occasion.

"See," said Katy, as Clover came into the room a little before tea-time, " Miss Pettingell has brought home my new dress. I'm going to wear it for the first time to go downstairs."

"How pretty!" said Clover, looking at the beautiful dove-coloured dress. "But Katy, I came up to shut your door. Bridget's going to sweep the hall, and I don't want the dust to fly in."

"What a strangetime to sweep a hall!" said Katy. "Why don't you make her wait till morning?"

"Oh, she can't! There are—she has—I mean there will be other things for her to do tomorrow. Don't worry, Katy, darling, but just keep your door shut. You will, won't you? Promise me!"

"Very well," said Katy, more and more amazed. "I'll keep it shut."

She took a book and tried to read, but the letters danced up and down before her eyes, and she couldn't help listening. Bridget was making the most awful noise with her broom, but through it all Katy seemed to hear other sounds—feet on the stairs, doors opening and shutting, once, a stifled giggle. How strange it all was!

"Never mind," she said to herself, "I shall know all about it tomorrow."

Tomorrow dawned fresh and fair—a perfect September day.

"Katy," said Clover, as she came in from the garden with her hands full of flowers, "that dress of yours is sweet. You never looked so nice before in your life. Father's coming up in a minute to take you down."

Just then Elsie and Johnnie came in. They had on their best frocks. So had Clover. Cecy followed, and then Dr Carr appeared.

Very slowly they all went downstairs, Katy leaning on her father, with Dorry on her other side, and the girls behind, while Philly clattered ahead. And there were Debby and Bridget and Alexander, peeping out of the kitchen door to watch her.

"Oh, the front door is open!" said Katy in a delighted tone. "How nice! And what pretty linoleum! That's new since I was here."

"Don't stop to look at *that*!" cried Philly, who seemed in a great hurry about something. "Come into the parlour instead. Don't wait, oh, don't wait!"

He seemed to be in an agony of impatience. So they moved on. Father opened the parlour door. Katy took one step into the room—then stopped. The colour flashed into her face and she had to hold on to the door to support herself. What was it that she saw?

Not just the room itself, with its fresh muslin curtains and vases of flowers. No, there was something else! The sofa was pulled out, and there upon it, her bright eyes

turned to the door, lay—Cousin Helen! When she saw
Katy she held out her arms.

Katy, forgetting her weakness, let go her father's arm,
and absolutely *ran* towards the sofa.

"Oh, Cousin Helen! Dear, dear Cousin Helen!" she
cried.

Then she tumbled down by the sofa somehow, the two
pairs of arms and the two faces met, and for a moment
or two not a word was heard from anybody.

"Isn't it a nice surprise?" shouted Philly. "It was Clover's idea. Cousin Helen's going to stay three weeks this
time. Isn't that nice?"

Katy thought that it was very nice indeed.

Such a short day that seemed! There was so much to
see, to ask about, to talk over, that the hours flew, and
evening dropped upon them all like another great surprise.

Cousin Helen was perhaps the happiest of the party.
It was clear to her that Katy had become the centre
and the sun of the whole family. Best of all, she saw the
change in Katy's face; the gentle expression of her eyes,
the womanly look, the pleasant voice, the politeness,
and the tact in advising the others without seeming to
advise.

"Dear Katy," she said a day or two after her arrival,
"this visit is a great pleasure to me—you can't think how
great. It's such a contrast to the last I made, when you
were so sick, and everybody so sad. Do you remember?"

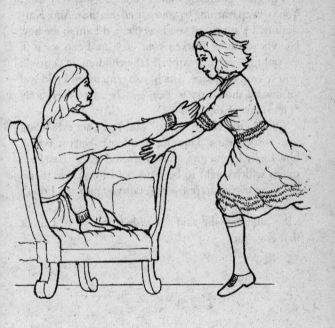

"Indeed I do. I remember too how good you were, and how you helped me. I shall never forget that."

"I'm glad, although what I could do was very little. You've been learning by yourself all this time. And, Katy darling, I want to tell you how pleased I am to see how bravely you have worked your way up. I can see it in everything—in your father, in the children, in yourself. You've won the place, which, you remember, I told you an invalid should try to gain—of being to everybody 'The Heart of the House'."

"Oh, Cousin Helen, don't!" said Katy, her eyes filling with sudden tears. "I haven't been brave. You can't think how badly I sometimes have behaved. Every day I see things which ought to be done, and I don't do them. It's good of you to praise me, but you mustn't. I don't deserve it."

But although she said she didn't deserve it, I think that Katy did!

Illustrated Chosen Classics
—— *Retold* ——

Titles available in this series: